"That murdered ATF agent?" Scarlett asked.

King swallowed. "We worked a case together a little over ten years ago. Before everything got complicated."

"Complicated." That single word seemed to answer everything she needed to know. "I'm sorry. Doesn't seem fair."

"Fair's got nothing to do with it." His response came harder, more bitter, than he'd meant it to. Because it wasn't fair that the cartel got away with murder—literally—and left families and partners holding the grief. "All the cartel has done is make me fight harder."

"I'm going to have to be careful, then." Scarlett brushed past him and wrenched the door wide open. Long hair caught against the shoulder of her vest, and King found himself wanting to untangle it. She held the door open for him.

One step was all it would take to bring him into her world. The DEA didn't play small, but private military contractors like Scarlett operated on a whole new level. And she wanted him to come along. "Why's that?"

Her mouth hitched at one side. "Seems anyone who partners up with you ends up dead."

K-9 GUARDIANS

NICHOLE SEVERN

Harlequin

INTRIGUE

To all the pups out there. You will be mine.

Harlequin®
INTRIGUE™

Recycling programs
for this product may
not exist in your area.

ISBN-13: 978-1-335-45728-8

K-9 Guardians

Copyright © 2025 by Natascha Jaffa

 Harlequin Enterprises ULC
22 Adelaide St. West, 41st Floor
Toronto, Ontario M5H 4E3, Canada
www.Harlequin.com

Printed in U.S.A.

Nichole Severn writes explosive romantic suspense with strong heroines, heroes who dare challenge them and a hell of a lot of guns. She resides with her very supportive and patient husband, as well as her demon spawn, in Utah. When she's not writing, she's constantly injuring herself running, rock climbing, practicing yoga and snowboarding. She loves hearing from readers through her website, www.nicholesevern.com, and on Facebook at nicholesevern.

Books by Nichole Severn

Harlequin Intrigue

New Mexico Guard Dogs

K-9 Security
K-9 Detection
K-9 Shield
K-9 Guardians

Defenders of Battle Mountain

Grave Danger
Dead Giveaway
Dead on Arrival
Presumed Dead
Over Her Dead Body
Dead Again

A Marshal Law Novel

The Fugitive
The Witness
The Prosecutor
The Suspect

Visit the Author Profile page at Harlequin.com

CAST OF CHARACTERS

Scarlett Beam—The security consultant wants only one thing: for her skill set to do good in the world. She's signed on with Socorro for that exact mission, but the fight she and King are bringing to the cartel's front door is far larger than she ever expected.

King Elsher—He just lost his partner. When his DEA case intersects with Scarlett's, he's taken aback by the vibrant redhead who laughs at his jokes while overturning every rock to get to the killer. Only, one wrong step has put them both in danger. Can King get justice...and keep them both alive?

Socorro Security—The Pentagon's war on drugs has pulled the private military contractors of Socorro Security into the fray to dismantle the *Sangre por Sangre* cartel...forcing its operatives to risk their lives and their hearts in the process.

Hernando Munoz—*Sangre por Sangre*'s lieutenant is planning a coup to overthrow the current leadership, and he's willing to kill whoever he has to in order to do it.

Granger Morais—Socorro's counterterrorism agent is haunted by the sins of his past and fears the future of his country with *Sangre por Sangre* at the helm. He'll do whatever it takes to make sure that doesn't happen...including putting Socorro Security at risk.

Chapter One

They were coming.

Scarlett Beam stared at the security feed longer than she should have. Seconds ticked off one by one, putting everyone in this building in more danger the longer she refused to move. She had to be sure. To confirm she wasn't seeing things coming off a twenty-four-hour shift.

Dust kicked up in front of the perimeter cameras and blocked out early morning sun coming up over the cliffs to the west. "Don't make me do this," she said to herself.

She couldn't make the call until she had visual confirmation. Her hand hovered over the alarm she'd hand-wired throughout the building. One press. That was all it would take to start an outright war. She licked at dry lips.

The dust cleared.

Revealing four fully loaded—and most likely bullet-proof—SUVs. Coming straight at Socorro's headquarters. Every cell in her body spiked with battle-ready tension.

Sangre por Sangre had crossed the line.

Scarlett slammed her hand down on the alarm. Ear-piercing shrieks urged operatives into action. She backed away from the security console built with her own two hands and reached for her sidearm. Compressing the release, she caught the magazine and inventoried the rounds stacked inside as she headed into the corridor. Low shouts echoed off black walls, tile, artwork and ceilings and drove her toward the armory.

It shouldn't have come to this. She thought they'd have more time.

Socorro Security's orders to dismantle the most bloodthirsty drug cartel in New Mexico had come straight from the Pentagon. A year of intelligence gathering, close calls and surveillance hadn't come close to an attack like this. Each organization knew the danger of provoking the other until the time was right. Seemed Sangre por Sangre had gotten tired of waiting.

Movement registered ahead as Socorro's counterterrorism agent dashed ahead of her. Two other operatives followed after as she rounded into the armory. They were private military contractors. Trained in war, weapons, strategy, combat and intelligence gathering throughout their military careers. Each of them moved with efficiency as they pulled high-powered rifles from mounts and stashed extra ammunition in their vests.

"What do we got, Scarlett?" Granger Morais holstered a backup pistol at his ankle. The former counterterrorism agent knew all about surprise attacks, having worked the investigation of 9/11 and the ambush on the American consulate in Benghazi. If they were going to get out of this alive, it would be because of him.

"Four vehicles, upgraded, one mile out. I'm not sure how many hostiles inside. Assume your rounds won't pierce the bodies or windows given Jones's run-in a couple weeks ago." Socorro's combat coordinator had barely survived the encounter as he'd tried to protect a war correspondent who'd gotten herself in the cartel's crosshairs. Scarlett strapped into her Kevlar as the tick of nails grew in intensity from the corridor. She really needed to trim those.

Competing *growls* told her the vet had sent out Hans and Gruber to back Scarlett up. The Dobermans charged into the armory, most likely having sniffed out her scent, and circled in tight rotations around her legs. The K9s had come from the same litter—brother and sister—and had learned to stick to Scarlett's every order since she signed on with the company. There wasn't anyone else she'd want at her side once they headed out into this mess.

"Damn it. They're getting ballsy. I'll give them that." Granger sheathed an oversize blade into the holster along his thigh. No matter the situation, he'd be prepared. That was what made him one of the best. What made them all the best. "All right. Cash, you and Jocelyn take the high ground. I want as many targets in your scopes as you can manage in case this goes sideways. Scarlett, you're with me in the welcome party. Bring the twins. They look like they haven't bit anyone in a while."

Cash Meyers—the operative charged with predicting the cartel's moves before Sangre por Sangre made them—dragged two heavy-duty cases from the steel shelf at the back of the room and handed one off to his equally experienced partner, Jocelyn Carville. "We need to alert Chief Halsey and the rest of Alpine Valley the cartel is in the area. Make sure all civilians shelter in place until the threat has passed."

"The alert was sent out the moment I hit the alarm.

I'm sure Alpine Valley PD is already issuing the order."
Because that was their job. To protect those who couldn't
protect themselves. It was why Scarlett had signed on
with Socorro in the first place. She secured her sidearm,
hand pressed along the grip. It'd been a long time since
she'd had to unholster her weapon, and that same dread
that accompanied the last time infiltrated her focus.

"Good. Then let's move." Granger took the lead, with
Cash and Jocelyn splitting off with their rifles slung over
their backs into a separate corridor.

Hans and Gruber kept on her heels as they weaved
through the maze meant to confuse and disorient un-
welcome visitors. Though Scarlett had done everything
in her power as Socorro's security expert to ensure that
never happened. Her gaze cut to the space where the
ceiling met the wall, where she'd hidden the backup
plan that would even any score should her team find
themselves cornered.

Speckles of dust glittered in front of her face as she
and Granger cut through the building's front lobby and
toward the double glass doors. Socorro's headquarters
had been set into the side of a mountain range in the
middle of the New Mexico desert. Why the structure
had a lobby at all—as though they were expecting visitors or potential clients—had never made sense to her.
But gratitude shifted through her at the added space between her and the outside world.

Granger paused before hitting the door release, that
unkempt swatch of facial hair hiding any tell around his
mouth. "You good?"

No. She wasn't. Injuries from two weeks ago still
pulsed, suffered from taking on a cartel member much

stronger and much bigger than her in an attempt to save Jones's journalist. But she wasn't about to back down. She hadn't before. She wouldn't start now. "I have one of Jocelyn's oatmeal bakes in the microwave. Let's get this over with so I can eat."

Granger's laugh took a bit of the uncertainty out of her nerves. He pushed through the doors and out into the open.

They moved as one, weapons raised as four SUVs skidded to a stop a mere twenty yards from the building. Sangre por Sangre had never before attempted to get this close.

Which meant something was very, very wrong.

Scarlett clocked Cash and Jocelyn taking up position on the roof, each tucked into their own corner for the best advantage. She and Granger were covered. No matter what happened next, her team had her back. And the Dobermans would eat anyone alive who tried to take her down. Sweat secreted around her grip and threatened to loosen her calm.

"Steady." Granger leveled his chin parallel to the ground with all the confidence and authority she didn't have. "We're not going to be the ones to shoot first. Understand? Anything that happens today, we want them to make the first move. That way, any retaliation is sanctioned by the Pentagon."

"Understood." Her voice shook on that single word, giving away the earthquake shuddering inside. This was her job. What she'd trained for. She was good at this, yet there was still a small part of her that wished she was stronger. More in control. Made better choices. Coming to Socorro—supporting her team, taking responsibility for others—was supposed to be her way to make up for the past, but she still couldn't shake the tremor in her hand.

Granger pulled up short. Waiting. The message was clear. One wrong move, and Socorro would do whatever it took to defend their territory.

Only the cartel didn't make that move.

Seconds split into minutes, into what felt like an hour, as the rising sun glinted off the SUV windshields.

Impatience undermined her forced calm. She really did have an oatmeal bake in the microwave, and her stomach wasn't too proud to admit its desperation for calories. "What are they waiting for?"

"I don't know." That wasn't like Granger. Certainty had always been one of the qualities she most admired the few times they'd been partnered on an assignment together, but this was something neither of them had experienced. Sangre por Sangre had always moved with compulsion rather than strategy. This...this was something else.

The hatch of one SUV raised behind the lead SUV. A dark, heavy tarp rolled out of the cargo area and hit the ground. Dust exploded from the impact and punctured Scarlett's resolve. She took a step forward. The Dobermans were ready to follow, but one throaty warning from Granger pulled them all up short. "What is that?" she asked.

The answer was already shoving to the front of her mind. Cartels like Sangre por Sangre lived for theatrics. Tires filled with accelerant and set on fire draped around victims' necks, raids on innocent towns, underage recruits, bombings of high-level law enforcement officers, soccer balls packed with nitroglycerin that exploded on impact in civilian parks. More recently, the abduction and torture of a war correspondent who'd seen too much.

The cartel's MO was bloody and violent and usually followed by weeks of media coverage. Sangre por Sangre's leadership wanted their name to be known, to be feared. It was domination, manipulation and control in the purest form. Because as long as the general public feared them, there was no one brave enough to stand up to fight them.

But Scarlett was. She had to be.

Engines caught, one after the other. Daytime headlights lit up as the SUVs backed away from the package and retreated. Billows of dirt scattered into the air, surely making it hard for Cash and Jocelyn to keep the targets in their sights.

Scarlett stared at the tarp. Willed it to move.

"Wait." Granger hugged his rifle close to his chest. The wear in his face was more evident than it'd ever been before. It was as though he'd aged a decade in the span of ten minutes.

This job… It was getting to him. To all of them. The constant threats, the need to be in the center of the action, the physical and mental scars that came with fighting an enemy a whole hell of a lot stronger and more violent than you. Who gained pleasure from hurting the very people you swore to protect. All she and Socorro had done was wait. And now the cartel had the upper hand.

"No. I'm tired of waiting." Scarlett took that first step, breaking Granger's order. Then another. She picked up the pace to a jog, then a flat-out sprint as she closed the distance between her and the elongated shape under the tarp. Her muscles ached as she pulled to a stop a few feet away.

Hans and Gruber dashed ahead, circling the package. A corner lifted on a dry breeze and gave her the first glimpse of what was inside.

A human hand.

She captured the tarp on the next gust and ripped it back as Granger stepped into her peripheral vision. But all Scarlett had attention for was the blade stabbed through a law enforcement shield and into the body's chest. Her stomach knotted tight. "He's a DEA agent."

HIS PARTNER WAS DEAD.

King Elsher stared down at the body, not really seeing the man unmoving on the examination table. Adam had gone missing three days ago. No activity on his credit cards. No outgoing calls from his cell phone. It was as though his best friend and partner of three years had up and vanished.

Only that wasn't true, was it?

Sangre por Sangre had finally found a way to get their message to King. Though why they'd delivered it to a private military contractor's doorstep, he had no idea.

The DNA, dental records and fingerprints all lined up. There was no denying his partner was the one lying here in the middle of the Alpine Valley morgue.

Cold air tightened the tendons in King's hand, making them ache. A blue papery sheet hid the stab wound centered in Adam's chest. Two inches in length, a few centimeters wide. Photos taken from the scene where his partner's body had been dumped showed the blade had gone through Adam's badge. Something that would've taken a lot more force than your average stabbing. This had been methodical. Purposeful, even.

"Do you have any questions, Agent Elsher?" The medical examiner—a guy who looked on the verge of retirement if it weren't for the fact he probably didn't have a cent to his name—stuffed thin hands into his white lab coat. Round wire-framed glasses slid down a beak-like nose, and the examiner scrunched up his face to put them back in place. Practiced. This was a guy used to multitasking when his hands were busy.

"Who found him?" That wasn't what he meant to ask. King had wanted to know if his partner had suffered. If he bled out in a slow crawl or if the blade did the job quickly.

But he already had the answer. Cartels like Sangre por Sangre—viruses that had no care for their hosts and fought against every vaccine in its path—didn't believe in mercy. They would've ensured Adam knew what was happening, felt it. For as long as possible.

The pathologist broke his statue-like observation and reached for a clipboard off to the side of the examination table. He flipped through a few pages. "There's a Scarlett Beam listed in the report. One of those private military contractors up at Socorro Security. I don't see any contact information, but I imagine you and the DEA know how to get in touch with her."

The DEA. Right. Because this was now an official investigation. Everything King had done to find a way into the cartel would come to light. There was no more hiding. No more unofficial requests or surveillance. No more covering his personal mission to dismantle the car-

tel on his own. Adam's case was about to expose him
in every way. Had that been Sangre por Sangre's plan?
To find a way to take King off the board? Hell. It would
work. Unless…

Socorro and private military contractors like them
had their own set of rules. They didn't answer to anyone but the Pentagon. The past few weeks had proven
that with coverage of a New Mexico state senator ac-
cused of using his own resources to render Socorro's
federal contract void, claiming the company was inten-
tionally letting Sangre por Sangre increase in size and
strength for the sole purpose of keeping operatives em-
ployed. The accusation lost its merit when a journalist
widely exposed the senator for working with the cartel
to achieve his goals.

If King played his cards right, Socorro could legitimize his investigation. Assuming Ivy Bardot and her
operatives wanted to know who'd ordered the murder
of a DEA agent as much as he did. Which, based off the
reports he'd read on the company's dealings with the
cartel, collaboration between their agencies was looking like a good option.

King scrubbed a hand down his face, taking in the
dry skin around Adam's eyes, the darker coloring of a
bruise settling along his partner's jaw. No. Sangre por
Sangre didn't get to slink back into the shadows and use
his partner as an example. Adam deserved better. His
family deserved better. And King was going to make
the people who'd done this paid. Starting with finding
Scarlett Beam. "Thanks, Doc. I'll be in touch."

He shoved through the double freezer-like doors sep-
arating the morgue from the rest of the building and hit

something solid on the other side. Red hair and a whole lot of tactical gear consumed his attention as the woman fell back from the impact.

King shot his hand out, catching hers to soften the blow. But the weight of her gear dragged him down with her. They landed on the tile floor with a smack. Pain ignited into his palm and through his wrist as he ended up pinning her against the floor. His breath shot free from his chest. "Oh, hell. I'm sorry. I didn't realize there was anyone of the other side of the door."

"You certainly know how to make an exit." She grabbed for the back of her head, pulling her hand back as though looking for blood. Three lines cut across the bridge of her nose in a wince. Right before she set intensely clear eyes on him. "You're welcome to get off of me anytime."

"Oh, right." King shoved to stand. Heat flared into his neck as he replayed the past few seconds over in his head. Nope. There was no rewriting this. No matter how many different ways he imagined it. Offering his hand to help her stand, he threaded the other through his hair. "Didn't realize the zombie apocalypse was already here. I should've come more prepared."

She didn't bother taking his hand as she got to her feet. Recentering her vest, she checked to ensure her sidearm was still holstered. A SIG Sauer. Preferred military issue. Instinct had him filling in the blanks. Without any military bases this far into the desert, there was only one conclusion to come to. She worked for Socorro Security.

Wide almond-shaped eyes lined with black and

framed by perfectly shaped eyebrows landed on him. "Sorry?"

"Your gear. The morgue." King hiked a thumb over his shoulder toward the swinging doors he'd effectively used to ruin her day. "This is as good a place as any to make sure there aren't any walking dead wandering around." Another wave of embarrassment undermined his social skills. King offered his hand. "Agent King Elsher. DEA."

She took his hand. Not at all as soft as he'd expected. As though she spent every day in the field rather than protected by shiny glass bulletproof windows. "Scarlett Beam. Socorro. And I figure it's better to be constantly alert for the zombie apocalypse rather than find myself in the middle of an ambush."

His laugh took him by surprise. A woman after his own heart.

"I take it you're here about the agent the cartel dropped off at my doorstep this morning," she said.

Tightness he'd always associated with the excitement of a lead knotted behind his sternum. Followed quickly by the dread pooling at the base of his spine. King released her hand as the latter won out. Reality punctured through the ignorance of the past few minutes. Hell. What was he going to tell his son Julien about today? How was a ten-year-old supposed to deal with the fact Adam wasn't going to be there anymore? "He was my partner. His name was Adam. Adam Dunkeld."

"I'm sorry, Agent Elsher." Sincerity laced the low register of her voice, and King suddenly had the thought of what his name would sound like on her lips. Which letter she would enunciate over all the others. "I'm sure you've read my statement Alpine Valley PD took at the scene. I'm here to check in with the medical examiner about any developments, but I'm happy to take a few minutes to answer any questions you might have."

"You're working the investigation." This was what he needed. What would save him in the end. Partnering with Scarlett could exonerate him in more ways than one. Could help him keep his job. And, hell, he needed this job. Suddenly finding himself a father of a ten-year-old kid he hadn't even known existed until two months ago came with a weight he hadn't expected. Financially, mentally, emotionally. He was still sorting through the responsibilities of being a father and how to balance his job with the first taste of a personal life. Working cases for the DEA—working to bring down the evil that threatened people's futures, like his son's—drove him to be the man he was. The kind of man Adam had been.

"No. There is no investigation. At least, not from my end. Socorro is a lot of things, but murder falls to local police and federal agencies." A shift in her weight told him how uncomfortable she was one-on-one. The kind of steel it took to be in the middle of the action—one that couldn't ever be forged on the sidelines—didn't like to stand still.

They were similar in that respect. He'd always been more inclined to get his hands dirty rather than push paperwork. Though now that he was approaching forty, past fractures and aches he'd acquired in the field took a bit longer to shake off.

"I just wanted…" She paused. "I wanted to know who he was. See how I could help the case."

She was right about the investigation. The DEA would partner with local police to stay up to date on Adam's murder, but ultimately, Alpine Valley PD would make every call and run every lead. Didn't matter that it was a federal agent who'd landed on the other side of these double doors. Seemed King had jumped the gun assuming Socorro would want in on the action. "I appreciate it."

"Did he have a family? Anyone waiting for him to come home?" Scarlett asked.

King had the urge to run for the door. To put as much distance between him and this place as he could. But running had never solved anything. And damn it, he was the reason Adam had been abducted and murdered in the first place. He owed his partner this. "Yeah. A wife, couple of kids, another one on the way."

"The medical examiner usually contacts next of kin." Scarlett nodded toward the big doors that'd taken her down. "But that's why you're here, isn't it? You want to be the one to tell them what happened. So you asked the ME to hold off on the notification."

How had she read him so easily? As though they'd known each other longer than a tackle to the floor and a potential concussion. "I was his partner," he said again.

"I understand," she said. "I've been where you are. Lost people I cared about."

He had to do this. For Adam. For himself. Hell, for his son's future where the cartel didn't haunt their dreams. And there was only one way to do it. Through Socorro.

King closed the distance between them, lowering his voice. "Then you know I'm going to do whatever it takes to find the person who stabbed him. Official or not."

She held her ground. Not the least bit intimidated by his intentions. A hint of curiosity filtered into her eyes. "All right, Agent Elsher. In that case, what can Socorro do for you?"

Chapter Two

She was going to catch hell for this.

Socorro was under scrutiny. Not only because of the past few weeks of media coverage that exposed a senator with a personal vendetta against her and her team but from the towns impacted by a military contractor's presence. Seemed every move Socorro made to save lives put others in more danger by antagonizing the cartel.

But Scarlett believed in the work. In keeping Sangre por Sangre and organizations like it from swallowing this state whole. It was because of her and her team that the fire hadn't burned out of control.

Picketers had set up beneath pop-up canopies of varying colors outside of Socorro's headquarters. She spotted them even this far out, and her grip tightened on the steering wheel as they carved along the one-lane dirt road leading straight home. Protestors wanted Socorro out of New Mexico. Convinced Socorro had brought the cartel straight to their doorstep, but the truth was, Sangre por Sangre had been there all along. Waiting. Preying on the innocent. Biding their time to make their moves from the dark. Socorro had only exposed them for what they really were. A sleeping disease no one could diagnose until it was too late.

Headquarters itself looked as though it'd come from space. All sharp corners, dark windows and mystery. At any moment, a large metal ramp could descend to reveal the alien occupants inside.

"Didn't realize you guys liked to throw parties." Agent Elsher—King—leaned forward in the front seat. She'd confirmed his credentials by cloning his phone to hers. Not exactly legal, considering he was a federal agent of the highest order, but she wasn't going to use the data against him. King Elsher, thirty-eight, served with the DEA for the past six years. Former cop from Seattle. Not a whole lot of activity in recent calls, but there'd been quite a change in his expenses over the past few months. A large increase in spending without anything to show for it. At least, not yet.

Something she'd have to dig into deeper when she had a few minutes to herself. Because that was where it started. Where the cartel liked to add pressure. It'd happened too many times than she wanted to count. Financials were the easiest way to corrupt even the best officers and agents. She once fought to give most people the benefit of the doubt, but she'd been burned one too many times.

"And here I'm just now finding out I wasn't invited," he said.

She tried to stop her mouth from hiking at one corner into a smile, but there was no stopping it. Despite her personal suspicions and need to unearth every small detail of a person's life before she trusted them, King was easy to talk to. Didn't hurt that they shared that same sarcastic and detached sense of humor, either. Like seeking like, and all that brain science. "Oh, yeah. It's a rager. Been going for weeks with no end in sight. I'm sure they wouldn't mind if you joined. They've been recruiting as many as they can into the We Hate Socorro fan club."

"The people here are really pissed, aren't they?" King distanced himself away from the window as Scarlett slowed to break through the growing crowd.

"They're scared. And with good reason. Seems every mission we carry out against Sangre por Sangre is returned tenfold," she said. "Only we're not the only ones who reap the consequences."

The herd had moved to stop her from entering the parking garage. Two operatives—she recognized Jones and Granger—took positions on either side of the entrance to ensure trespassers couldn't slip in unnoticed. Her teammates faced off with the verbal assaults without so much as responding.

Someone hit their hand against the back window of Scarlett's SUV. Then another. Each punctured deep through her nervous system and spiked her heart rate.

Posters with crude writing demanded Socorro leave while others threatened individual agents. Since the senator's accusations two weeks ago, every one of these people had taken up the mantle to protect themselves the best way they could. No matter how illogical their strategy.

"But fear can be far more dangerous than any perceived threat," Scarlett said.

King didn't have an answer to that.

Scarlett heaved a sigh of relief as she maneuvered the SUV down into the belly of the garage. Darkness slipped over the windshield, suddenly making the cabin that much more intimate. Without her full vision, her senses picked up on other things. Like how King had set his arm on the center console dividing their seats. Even the slight hint of dirt and cologne she'd gotten a lungful of when he'd fallen on top of her in the morgue seemed more intense. Not entirely unpleasant.

No. Wait. That might be coming from her vest after he tackled her.

"You sure you still want to get involved with Socorro?" She pulled the vehicle in front of the elevators and cut the engine. Shouldering out of the SUV, she hit the pavement and strode to the keypad she had personally upgraded as soon as the picketers set up shop outside. The garage door rolled to a close at the head of the ramp, both of her teammates now inside. "We're not exactly popular right now. Could kick back onto you and the DEA."

King met her at the keypad, the tendons linked between his neck and shoulders strung tight. She'd talked with him long enough to understand he was in unknown territory, putting his career on the line. Why else would he turn to Socorro rather than the DEA? "I don't have any other choice."

This wasn't about competing with local law enforcement for jurisdiction over his partner's investigation. There was something more he wasn't telling her. Something only she could give him. Hesitation closed in around her throat. She'd been used once before. She wasn't eager to experience it a second time. Scarlett pressed her hand onto the print reader. The elevators engaged, their polished shiny silver doors parting down the middle. She motioned him inside the car. "After you."

They took the elevator to the fourth floor and stepped out into a cavern of black. The cameras she'd installed in every corner catalogued more than their faces. Her top-of-the-line security analyzed body heat, a person's walk and homed in on any weapons they might be carrying. Which, around her, was usually a lot. Ivy Bardot would know they were coming. There wasn't a single detail that woman missed inside this building or out.

"You have to give me the number of your decorator." King seemed to be taking everything in but most especially the locations of each of her cameras and which turns they made away from the elevators. Planning for an escape. Just as she would. "I never thought black on black could be so…"

"Absurd? Yeah, me neither. At least not until I moved in here." Scarlett guided him around one corner and toward the penthouse office at the end of the corridor.

It was odd, having someone to talk to while she walked these halls. Like she'd invited King into her personal space. Every inch of these walls had felt her touch as she ensured nothing could hurt her and her team. She was the only one who preferred to stay in the building, out of sight. It was where she did her best work.

"Operatives live here." A hint of disbelief crept into his voice, and it was under these too-bright florescent lights that Scarlett finally got a good look at King Elsher. Not encumbered by a possible concussion or the limited view in the SUV.

Lean muscle banded around his neck and sprawled down into his chest. He took care of himself, that much was clear. His T-shirt—far more worn than she would have expected—kept the last few remnants of a design over his heart. But whether he wore it for its personal connection or because he couldn't afford anything newer, she didn't know. That was where an audit of his finances would come in handy. Light-colored hair had been closely shaved up the sides of his head, leaving a mop of controlled curls at the top. He'd retained a sense of boyishness in his features, soft in some areas. Around his mouth, for example. But experience had hardened the skin and shape of his eyes.

"Voluntarily?" he asked.

"Makes the most sense for us. My team takes shifts where we're on call twenty-four-seven. So we each have a bedroom with a connected bathroom, we share a communal kitchen. Though one of my teammates will gut you with a whisk if you try to mess anything up in there and probably smile while doing it. We have a theater room for downtime, an on-call physician in case of emergency, a gym with every machine known to man and a food delivery service. Even a vet who takes care of our K9s. We have everything we need." Scarlett heard the pride in her own voice. Out of all the places she could've ended up after her last tour, Socorro was the only one that'd thrown her a lifeline. For her, this was more than she deserved. "We're all former military. We like to be ready when we're needed."

"So what you're saying is, you live inside your own end-of-the-world bunker, and you're preparing to take over the world without ever having to leave." King nodded in appreciation. "I like it."

"Stick around long enough, I'll introduce you to Hans and Gruber." She shoved through the conference room door, holding it open for him over the threshold.

Confusion warped those handsome features. He lowered his voice. "Is that code for…you know." He nodded to her chest. "Because I should tell you I'm not really in a position for a relationship right now. My partner was just found murdered, and—"

"Agent Elsher." Ivy Bardot stepped out from behind the conference room table. "As interesting as your relationship status is, I think there are more important topics we should discuss."

Granger's failed attempt to keep his laugh to himself filled the room.

Scarlett couldn't stop the appreciation for this moment or the deep flush of embarrassment coloring King's neck and face as he dared a step into the conference room. She was going to remember him. For a long time. She let the door automatically close behind them. "King, meet the founder and CEO of Socorro. Ivy Bardot. And this is Granger Morais, our resident counterterrorism expert."

"Why do I suddenly feel like I'm being brought into the principal's office?" King nodded at each in turn instead of extending his hand. He seemed to memorize everything about this room and the people in it.

"Because you know as well as we do, you're not supposed to be here, are you, Agent Elsher?" Ivy took her position at the head of the table and motioned for King to take a seat. An offer he didn't accept. "You and your team work cartel cases from a drug standpoint. You don't get involved in homicide investigations, even those of your agents. Which means the DEA doesn't know you're here."

Scarlett battled the dread pooling at the base of her spine.

"You're right. My superiors have no idea I'm here," King said. "I came because I've been investigating a Sangre por Sangre lieutenant for the past eight months. Off the record and with DEA resources. Now that investigation has gotten my partner killed."

HIS CAREER—his whole life and that of his son's—was suddenly in someone else's hands. King didn't like the idea of not being able to choose his own path.

The pressure of those seconds as Socorro's founder stared back at him, unblinking, felt as though he were right back in the moment when a social worker had showed up on his doorstep and dropped off a ten-year-old kid King hadn't known existed.

Then again, he'd been the one to bring himself to this point. In both scenarios.

He'd been the one to go home with a woman he barely knew for more than a couple hours a little over a decade ago. It'd been mutual, a way for him and a visiting ATF agent he'd been partnered with during an investigation to blow off some steam, and he hadn't regretted that choice for a single moment. Until two months ago. Now he had Julien, and he didn't know how to take care of a kid, but they were trying to make it work. Little by little. Day by day. Fruit snack by fruit snack.

"Will you help me?" Because Socorro was the only thing that could save him now. This group of military contractors who seemed to trust each other more than King even trusted himself. He had nowhere else to go. No one who could justify his actions of the past eight months of looking into Sangre por Sangre unsanctioned. And the minute he was exposed, he'd lose everything.

He'd be arrested and charged. His career would be over. The state would take his son.

A burning lodged in his chest at the mere thought. King wasn't going to let that happen.

Awareness spiked as Scarlett's warmth seeped into his arm. A trick. Experience told him it was just a game his mind was trying to play on him, a way to connect with the very people who could dismantle his life. But a part of him wanted that sincerity she seemed to put into every word and every expression to be true.

"You want Socorro to corroborate your unsanctioned investigation into the cartel." Ivy Bardot lived up to her reputation. Smarter than those bureaucrats on Capitol Hill wanted her to be and definitely out of their league. She wasn't just playing the game. She was calling the shots, and the federal government would only take so many commands before turning to bite the hand that fed them cartels like Sangre por Sangre. "Who is your target?"

Hope jumped in his chest where it had no right to land. "Hernando Muñoz."

"We know the name. Intel says he took a hard leap to the top of the cartel's hierarchy once the Big Guy's only son was found with a bullet between the eyes. Making quite a name for himself, too. Violently." Morais—the counterterrorism agent—set his elbows on the conference table, a quiet intensity churning in the space between them. As though waiting for the perfect time to ambush. "Guy's a thug. Hangs out with a trusted group of cartel members, but we've never been able to link him to any of the drug activity in the area. Any business we suspect he's involved in is divided between his crew. Totally hands-off. Our team's got surveillance, but all we've managed to gather is he likes takeout almost every night of the week, and he buys his wife a lot of flowers. So I'm curious. What do you have on him?"

"Nothing." King smothered the hope he'd stupidly allowed himself to feel. "All I've got is rumors Muñoz is stirring up trouble from within. Getting ready for a takeover. And you're right. He's careful, and none of his crew is willing to talk. He makes sure he never touches the money that comes his way from his guys working corners, but I don't care about the drugs or what kind of pies he's got his fingers in on the cartel's behalf. I have reason to believe he ordered the murder of an ATF agent who was getting too close to his operation two months ago. The investigators couldn't come up with anything conclusive, but I know Muñoz is involved. Just like I know he's responsible for Adam's murder." His tongue felt too big for his mouth as his personal life bled into his professional. "She was a good agent. And a good mom."

"You knew her." Scarlett's voice eased through him as slick as chocolate syrup.

There it was again. That uncanny ability she had to practically read his mind. King didn't have the guts to face her head-on, not trusting his ability to keep his emotions capped right then. "When it comes to Sangre por Sangre, we all know someone who's been hurt."

That was starting to look like his own personal motto.

The knot in his gut tightened as Ivy Bardot studied him for a series of breaths. Leaning back in her chair, Socorro's founder shoved to stand. "Send me your investigation notes. I want to know every detail of your operation, what resources you've used and what you have on Muñoz. We can't step on law enforcement's toes during your partner's homicide investigation, but if you're right about the lieutenant's intentions and what he's done, we'll need to put together a strategy. One that makes it look like you've been working with Socorro these past two months."

King barely had the sense to take his next breath.

"Scarlett, get with Agent Elsher and familiarize yourself with the ATF agent's murder. The case is closed, so you shouldn't have any pushback from police. Reach out to Chief Halsey from Alpine Valley PD, if needed, and bring me something concrete we can use to reopen the case and connect it with Adam Dunkeld's," Ivy said. "Granger, I want up-to-date information from the surveillance team. Patterns, logs, movements, identities of Muñoz's crew and everything you have on the wife. All of it."

Time seemed to speed up.

"You're going to corroborate my investigation," King said. "Why?"

The question seemed to slow down Socorro's founder. Something he was sure she wasn't used to. "Because I don't want it to be true, Agent Elsher. I don't want to believe that when it comes to Sangre por Sangre and cartels like it that we all know someone who's been hurt. Because if that's the case, then Socorro hasn't been doing its job, and innocent lives have been sacrificed for nothing."

He didn't know what to say to that. What to think. To the point, King didn't even bother getting out of Ivy Bardot's way as she maneuvered around him and shoved through the conference room doors. "She takes her job seriously, doesn't she?"

"Operatives like us don't have a choice, Agent Elsher. There are too many good people counting on us to come through for them. I'm sure you and the DEA know that better than anyone." Granger Morais got to his feet with a bent manila file folder in one hand. He headed for the door, smacking the file into King's shoulder on the way out. "Bring us something solid. We'll have your back."

"I appreciate that." It took longer than it should have for the past few minutes to sink in, but King couldn't let the time slip away too easily. He'd already wasted two months of hard work trying to do this on his own. Now he had an entire team willing to help him bring Muñoz to justice. He turned to face Scarlett. "Looks like we're going to be working together."

"That ATF agent. The one whose murder you suspect Muñoz ordered. Were you partners?" she asked.

King had to swallow the urge to shut down this line of questioning. He'd gotten what he wanted: support in pinning two murders on the son of a bitch who'd ordered the deaths of an ATF agent and now a DEA agent and an entire security firm to corroborate his personal investigation to do so. Scarlett wasn't asking to dig into his life. She needed the facts of the investigation to connect it all back to Muñoz. "We worked a case together a little over ten years ago. She was called in from DC to help my team analyze a device we picked up during a raid on one of the cartel's safe houses. Before everything got complicated."

"Complicated." That single word seemed to answer everything she needed to know, but Scarlett didn't push it. "Can I assume you believe these two murders are connected based off of MO?"

"Muñoz has a pension for making an example out of anyone who gets in his way. A knife through a law enforcement badge gets the point across, don't you think?" he asked.

"Even so, I'm going to need her name and the complete investigation file." Scarlett seemed to produce a tablet out of nowhere.

"Her name was Eva Roday." That last syllable caught in the back of this throat. It'd been months since he'd had the guts to say her name out loud. Especially around Julien. "As for the file, you'll have it within the hour. Washington DC detectives closed the case three weeks ago. We shouldn't have any problem getting access."

Scarlett countered the added distance between them. "I'm sorry. That you've had to go through this more than once. Doesn't seem fair."

"Fair's got nothing to do with it." His response came harder, more bitter, than he meant it to. Because she was right. It wasn't fair. It wasn't fair that the cartel got away with murder—literally—and left kids and families and partners and wives holding the grief all to themselves. Sangre por Sangre had taken the most important person his son had in the world, and even having known about him for only a short amount of time, there wasn't anything King wouldn't do to try to fix it. That was what fathers did, didn't they? Fix things. "All the cartel has done is make me fight harder. They're the ones who are going to wish I played fair in the end."

"I'm going to have to be careful then." Scarlett brushed past him, wrenching the swinging glass door wide open. Long hair caught against the shoulder of her vest, and King suddenly found himself wanting to untangle it. She leveraged her foot against the bottom and held the door open for him.

One step. One leap of faith was all it would take to bring him into her world. The DEA didn't play small, but Socorro? Private military contractors like Scarlett operated on a whole new level. And she wanted him to come along. "Why's that?"

Her mouth flattened into a thin line. "Seems anyone who partners up with you ends up dead."

Chapter Three

There wasn't anything she could do to take the pain out of his eyes.

But the internal drive she fed more often than not—the one that'd led her to Socorro—told her this was how she bought back her right to be here instead of a dark hole where she was referred to as a number instead of by her name. How she got rid of the guilt slowly eating away at her from the inside.

Scarlett dragged her finger from the bottom of her tablet screen up to review the file that hit her inbox a few minutes ago. Eva Roday's murder file.

Reaching for a steady breath, she tried to take in the overwhelming amount of information stuffed into one document. The detective who'd investigated the ATF agent's death had done a good job interviewing everyone in her life. Every detail seemed to jump out. Including the fact her ten-year-old son, Julien, had been left behind after her death. Her mouth dried. "Give me the basics."

"Agent Roday—Eva—was found with a blade similar to the one the ME pulled out of Adam this morning in the morgue." King settled that lean frame against the counter across from her in the too-small galley kitchen, a mug of fresh coffee in hand.

He needed it from the look of him. Dark circles had deepened past exhaustion and straight into night of the living dead. He'd run his hands through his hair one too many times, breaking up the careful sections of curls. The DEA agent with the eyes of steel turned out to be human after all.

"Six inches, serrated, with a patterned carbon fiber handle. No fingerprints left on the blade or the handle, but the medical examiner did manage to pull DNA off one of the blade's teeth. Problem is, they have nothing to compare it to."

Scarlett lost her grip on composure as the first crime scene photo filled her tablet screen. The spike in her heart rate could've been heard from across the room, she was sure of it, and she couldn't help but look up at King for confirmation. She tightened her hands around the edge of the screen. Pressure led to nausea, and a surge of acid tried choking her from within.

Patterned tile—new from the looks of it—supported the body as a pool of blood slipped out from the wound in the woman's chest. Cotton pajamas soaked up a lot of it. Not a suit. Nothing to suggest Eva Roday had been in the field during her murder. No. Whoever had done this came into her home. Located her badge, positioned it over the agent's chest and plunged the blade straight through. "She was found in her own home. Who called it in?"

"Her son. Julien," King said. "He's ten."

His voice did that. Caught on names. She'd noticed it earlier, and Scarlett couldn't help but imagine him doing the same with hers. Not with her last name as everyone addressed her. As Scarlett.

King crossed one ankle over the other. So relaxed in this place, somewhere he'd never even stepped before. That confidence bled off of him and settled deep in her bones. "The detective who caught the case didn't get a whole lot out of him that night. Medics couldn't find anything physically wrong with him, but…"

"You think he was there. That he saw what the killer did to his mother." Her heart constricted at the thought. There were some things in this world no one should ever have to see. Least of all the person you loved most in the world taken from you so brutally.

"Police found him beneath a pile of towels on the couch not five feet from where they found Eva's body. The killer would've done his research before stepping foot inside an ATF agent's house. He would've known she had a kid, and the son of a bitch went there anyway." King stared down into his coffee mug. The drop in his voice told her he was trying for detached—same as she was—but there was no amount of distance that could calm the rage boiling in that tone. "They thought Julien might've been injured, given the amount of blood on him, but none of it came back as his."

"He tried to save his mother?" Scarlett kept scrolling. To drain the dread growing in the pit of her stomach. To give herself something to do. A distraction. It didn't help. Because beside the agent's body was a too-small handprint. Made with blood.

"Yeah. He did." King set down the mug. There was no point trying to force it down when you couldn't physically stomach the aftermath of a case like this. Something he had to live with every day working for the DEA, she imagined. "Julien has been nonverbal ever since that night. He can't or won't tell police what he saw, if he noticed anything specific about the killer or the order of events. He's been seeing a child psychologist for the past two months, speech therapists, you name it. They all say the same thing. He understands his mom isn't coming back. He knows he can help police find her killer, but there isn't anyone in this world who can make him speak up until he's ready."

"Trauma-induced mutism." Scarlett made a note straight into the investigation file to read up on the symptom. Because it was something to do. A possible way she could help should she have to sit down with Julien. "It says here Agent Roday wasn't married. I don't see any beneficiaries for her life insurance or bank accounts listed other than Julien. Do you know anything about his father? Where he might be or if there were any hard feelings between him and the victim?"

King's expression hardened in an instant. "They hadn't had any contact in over a decade. He didn't even know Julien existed until Eva was killed and he was questioned by DC police. The detective cleared him of any involvement seeing as how the father was on assignment two hundred miles away. I'd say he's not pertinent to this investigation."

"Okay. Well, it's been two months." Scarlett mapped out a quick order of to-dos. "If he got custody of Julien, there's a chance we might be able to reinterview the boy—"

"No." That single word was a bark from across the kitchen. Aimed directly for her. King seemed to catch himself. The tendons along his neck and shoulders dropped away from his ears, but there was no hiding the truth. Protectiveness. He cared about Agent Roday's son. "I already told you Julien isn't talking. He's in a better place now. He's made friends at schools. His nightmares are becoming less frequent. Bringing all of this up might undo that, and I don't want to take that chance."

Her chin wobbled slightly, out of her control. It wasn't the aggression that'd caught her off guard. She lived and operated with an entire team of testosterone on the brink of blowing up in her face. She was trained to neutralize any threat—physical or digital—but King's intensity felt personal. As though she'd hit some kind of button he'd tried to hide away. "I understand."

"Good." He dumped his still-hot coffee into the sink and headed for the corridor that ran parallel to the kitchen. "I have copies of Eva's files. The last few cases she was working right before she died. I've been through them a thousand times, but there might be something in there you can pick up on."

"I wasn't finished." Scarlett lowered her tablet to her side as King slowed to a halt. The intensity she'd witnessed had simmered. Still there, but not burning out of control as before. Replaced with a kind of isolation, a loneliness she recognized every time she caught a reflection of herself in the bathroom mirror. "I understand why you wouldn't want to re-traumatize a ten-year-old boy by interviewing him about his mother's murder, but if you want me to help you find whoever killed Agent Roday and who killed your partner, you're going to have to be honest with me. Otherwise, your deal with Socorro ends here."

King didn't look at her, didn't even seem to breathe.

"Every time you talk about Agent Roday, you call her by her first name. Which means you knew her as more than a colleague you were teamed up with ten years ago." The pieces were starting to fit together. His personal investigation into the cartel that started two months ago, why he wanted to see his partner's body at the morgue for himself. Why he wouldn't want Scarlett or anyone else stepping foot near Julien. "And based off of your defensiveness about her son, how old he is and how well you seem to know him, I'm guessing there's a good reason for that."

The fight seeped from King's arms and shoulders. "I didn't lie before. Eva was called into analyze a device we found during one of the DEA's cartel raids on Sangre por Sangre. We worked well together in the field. She was smart as hell, to the point I tried to recruit her to work for us. Told her the cartel would roll over the second we brought her on, but she was happy in DC with the ATF. Had a whole life there, but the truth was there was something about her I wanted more of."

Scarlett braced herself against the obvious grief he'd held on to after all these years. Not just from Agent Roday's death, but from losing her in the first place ten years ago.

"Once our case was finished, we went out to celebrate with a couple drinks. One thing led to another, and in the morning, she was gone. Back to DC." A scoff escaped up his throat. "No goodbyes. No note. Nothing. I reached out a couple times but never heard anything from her again. Until two months ago when a ten-year-old boy who looks exactly like her shows up on my doorstep with a social worker in tow. She tells me Eva is dead and that I'm responsible for Julien now. That I'm his father."

Her blood pressure spiked. "You had no idea?"

"None at all." Life breathed into his rigid frame as King turned to face her. Devastation—so familiar and gutting—carved into his handsome face. "Listen, I know you're just trying to do the thing that makes the most sense. Talking to the only witness who was there the night of Eva's murder is standard protocol, but that little boy is finally coming to terms with having his entire world ripped away from him."

He took a step toward her. "And I won't let you or anyone else mess with that. He's my son, and I'm going to do whatever it takes to protect him."

HIS SON.

He wasn't sure he'd ever said the words out loud. Not in passing. Not even to Julien. Pathetic, wasn't it? His entire world had shifted in the course of weeks, but he hadn't even been able to put a name as to why. Until today.

King checked his smartwatch for the dozenth time. They weren't getting anywhere with Eva's investigation file. They sure as hell couldn't prove Muñoz was even remotely connected to her murder or to Adam's today. And now he had mere minutes before he had to be back in Albuquerque for school pickup.

This was his life now. He'd gone from pulling all-nighters and chasing every lead until he had nothing left, to cutting his days short in time to make sure Julien would see a familiar face when he got home. It was an adjustment. One King was still trying to get used to.

It wasn't about him anymore. Hell, none of this was. It was about giving his son a future free of fear, of suffering and maybe a little bit of justice in the process.

He scanned through Eva's file for the thousandth time. Nothing had changed. No light bulb moments or new leads. He wasn't sure what he'd been hoping to uncover with Scarlett's help. Just…something.

King scrubbed his face. They were out of time. He checked his watch again.

"You keep doing that," she said.

Scarlett was everything he'd expected from a Socorro operative, but at the same time nothing like he'd imagined. She'd read through the investigation file without so much as a change in expression, which made King wonder what horrors she'd seen to make this case seem like basic training. The woman hadn't slowed down for a minute, charging through page after page. Photo after photo. Hadn't even stopped to eat. She was dedicated. He'd give her that. Either that, or a straight up workaholic.

"Checking your watch," she went on. "Either you've got some place to be, or I'm not living up to your ideals of a good partner."

"School pickup." He shoved to stand.

The conference room they'd taken over looked like the aftermath of a back to school warehouse sale. Note cards, highlighters, reports discarded across the oversize table. Felt like he was back in college cramming for an exam in a class he hadn't shown up to all semester.

Drug cases were simple. The crap they pulled off of street corners could be traced. Find the exact combination of poison and trace it back to a dealer. Force the dealer to flip on the supplier, then do it over and over again until there wasn't anyone left. The cartel would fall the same way, but homicide?

Ivy Bardot had been right. He didn't know how to do this.

King grabbed his jacket from the back of his chair. "If I leave now, I'll only be five minutes late. Which is better than my fifteen to thirty minutes late most days."

Scarlett shoved straight out of her chair and stretched. Her shirt slipped free from the front of her cargo pants as she reached overhead. A dark line cut across her abdomen. Jagged. As wide as a pencil eraser, but before King had a chance to follow it to the end, she was pushing her chair back under the table. "I'll drive you."

"Not sure if you know this, but DEA agents are trained and licensed to operate motor vehicles," he said.

"Did you forget I'm the one who brought you out here?" Scarlett gathered the file spread across the table back into a single stack, crisscrossed in sections for easy access.

Oh, hell. He'd left his SUV back at the morgue. And he didn't have time to get it. King threaded his arms into his jacket. "Yes. Yes, I did."

"Then let's go. I just have to make a quick stop." Her smile flashed wide, and an instant jolt shifted in his gut. There was something light and genuine about that smile that didn't make sense in their line of work. Something she should've lost a long time ago.

She took the lead through the maze until they landed at a nondescript door. "Brace yourself. Meeting the twins for the first time can be a little overwhelming."

"The twins?" King didn't get an answer before Scarlett shoved through the door. A low howl jogged his nerves as all hell broke loose. Two dark-haired Dobermans sprinted straight at him, teeth bared.

"Sit." One word from Scarlett, and the dogs pulled up short, planting their butts on the tile. Bright pink tongues licked at sharp teeth ready to sink into whatever could fit in their mouths, and King had no trouble imagining his arm made a good chew toy in their eyes.

King eased his hand over his sidearm, keeping an eye on the devils. "What is happening? Are these monsters yours?"

"This is Gruber and his sister Hans." Scarlett crouched, putting her face between theirs, but King couldn't help but notice while the Dobermans kissed at her face and neck, they kept their gazes solely on him. She scratched behind their ears. "They're defensive K9s. Any hint of a threat to me or the people in this building, they respond with force."

"What you're saying is, it's their job to eat people." King suddenly had the urge to unholster his weapon, but doing so might be seen as an act of aggression.

"Yeah." Scarlett stood, and the Dobermans fell in line on either side of her. "I'm their trainer, so don't piss me off."

His throat dried. A minute later, they wound their way to the elevator after a series of lefts and rights King lost track of halfway, all the while keeping his distance from Jekyll and Hyde. Truth be told, he couldn't tell which way was up in this place.

"How does anyone manage to navigate through the building? It all looks the same," he asked.

"I designed it that way in case of a breach." They

stepped into the elevator car and faced off with their reflections as the doors closed. "Disorienting the enemy can be useful in times of war. That, and a few other security measures I built in."

His stomach launched higher in his chest as gravity lost its hold during their descent into the garage. King had the instinct to reach out for Scarlett's shoulder to steady himself, but grabbing a coworker—in any field—could land him facedown with a knee in his back. Not to mention a couple flesh wounds. He closed his eyes and breathed through the disorientation. He needed a distraction. "I take it you served."

"Army. Security specialist." Her voice echoed off the walls of the elevator car. Steady, reassuring. If something were to happen right now, she'd be the one to know what to do. "Twelve years, three tours and partridge in a pear tree."

Impressive. Twelve years, though. Meant she hadn't served a full twenty and gotten her retirement like most of the vets he worked with in the DEA.

The nausea receded as the elevator landed in the garage. He pried his eyes open before taking that first step from the car after Scarlett. The scent of gasoline infiltrated his lungs and hauled him back into the moment. He'd gone all day without eating. Any longer and his blood sugar would get the best of him. "Is that where you got the scar?"

Scarlett pulled up short, and the Dobermans followed suit. A hint of betrayal contorted her expression. Just for a moment before she wiped her face of emotion. "Don't ask me about the scar, Agent Elsher. Not ever."

She didn't wait for an answer, heading for the nearest

SUV. The alarm chirped as they approached, and she got behind the steering wheel without waiting for him to catch up. The dogs climbed over her lap and went straight for the cargo area at the back. As though they'd done it a thousand times before.

Every interaction they'd had since he tackled her in the morgue opposed her reaction a few seconds ago. King made his way to the passenger seat and buckled in as she navigated through the garage.

Picketers rushed to his side of the vehicle. Neon signs written with barely legible handwriting and exclamation points. Yells filtered through the tinted glass. Blinding desert sun enveloped them as they left the safety of Socorro's headquarters, and suddenly he felt as though he'd screwed it all up. Just as he had those first couple weeks after Julien came to live with him. "I'm sorry. It was none of my business. It won't happen again."

The seconds ticked off one after another as they carved through the dry landscape, and King couldn't help but wish they could go back to how it'd been before he opened his mouth. "So does this mean we're going to be all awkward and standoffish with each other from now on?"

A whisper of that smile he'd witnessed in the conference room made an appearance and released the pressure strangling his insides. "Probably. Guess it's a good thing this arrangement is temporary."

He'd missed this over the past few days. Having someone to bicker with. When it came right down to it, working drug cases and chasing down leads took a toll. The things he'd seen in the field would stay with him forever, but being able to joke and laugh systematically released the darkness that accrued inside. Something he never wanted his son to see.

Adam had given him that for a while. Now King wasn't sure what would happen.

"Why Socorro?" he asked.

Scarlett checked the rearview mirror. "What do you mean?"

"The cartel dumped my partner's remains outside of your headquarters. Why not at his home or the DEA?" He pried his phone from his jacket pocket. Sixteen missed calls. A handful from his superior, the rest from Adam's wife.

She deserved answers. She deserved to know the truth. He'd convinced the medical examiner he should be the one to notify Adam's family of his death, but he'd been so caught up in going back through Eva's case looking for a connection, he'd managed to put it off as long as possible. King wasn't sure if the same applied to the DEA. If the media got hold of the story and broke the news first, he'd never be able to face Adam's wife and kids again.

His thumb hovered over the screen. One tap. That was all it would take to give her the relief she needed.

"I've been wondering that myself," Scarlett said. "You haven't told the family your partner was murdered."

"I've tried at least a dozen times, but there's not really a Hallmark card for that, is there? Nothing I could say that would make this any better." King pocketed his phone. He would do it. He'd make the call. But now wasn't the time. Not until he could assure her he'd gotten justice for Adam. Though he was sure his wasn't the only number she'd dialed the past few hours after not getting an answer from her husband. "'Sorry, I got your husband killed. My thoughts are with you.'"

"Just keep it simple. And mean what you say. It makes all the difference." Scarlett turned that intense green gaze on him.

"You have to deliver a lot of bad news in your line of work?" It was a stupid question and completely on the line of procrastination. He couldn't avoid the call forever. At this point, he was just making excuses.

"No, but I've been on the receiving end more times than I can count." Scarlett maneuvered through the neighborhood surrounding his son's elementary school as though she'd been here before. "We're here. Where is your son waiting?"

King sat up straighter in his seat, all thoughts of his partner's family draining as he searched for his own. Checking the time, he confirmed they weren't much later than his normal arrival. There were still a couple kids hanging around on the playground equipment soaking up a few more minutes with friends. Parents waiting in vehicles too. "He's supposed to be at the corner. Probably went into the office to wait. I'll be right back."

He shouldered out of the vehicle and jogged to the double glass doors beside the kindergarten area. The first layer of doors opened without issue, but he had to be buzzed into the office. He waited until the administrator unlocked the barrier. "Hi, I'm here to pick up Julien Roday. I'm his dad, King Elsher."

"Oh. There must've been some kind of mix-up on your end," she said. "Julien was checked out a couple hours ago."

No. That wasn't right. "Checked out? By who?"

The administrator collected the clipboard from her desk and handed it off. "By his mother."

Chapter Four

The water bottle exploded on impact mere inches from her face as she and King waited in a conference room off the school's main office.

Droplets sprayed out from the impact zone against the wall and attached to her skin, but she wouldn't wipe them away. They were evidence of a man's descent into desperation. She needed them to keep her focused.

King's son had been kidnapped.

Her heart rate hit a high point as he turned to face whoever had come through the door. Ready to unleash all that burning rage on the nearest unsuspecting witness. His shoulders hiked with tension, almost painful to look at, but in a split second, the anger drained.

King sank into one of the chairs around the too-small conference room. Nothing like Socorro's. Not in size, at least, but the work done in this space was just as important to the families that needed this school. "They took my son, Scarlett."

"We're going to find him." It was easy to match his tone. Her chest felt too tight at the thought of someone coming in here, claiming to be Julien's mother and walking away with King's son in order to punish a man for doing his job. Hadn't he been through enough? "The administrator at the front desk checked the woman's ID when she requested to check him out. She remembers the name matched Eva's. But it looks as though when the school in Washington, DC, transferred his records, there was no note about Eva's death. Her name is still attached to his records. I sent the district the death certificate to have that information changed."

That was all she could think to do while King raged. The principal had contacted the police. Officers were searching the school property and the surrounding neighborhood, but whoever took Julien wouldn't stick around. They wanted him for something, and it would be hell to get him back.

"He's ten years old." The strangled words sounded practically forced from his throat.

And she understood that. The amount of effort it took to confront your greatest fear. To realize that despite your training, you were absolutely powerless when the people you loved were in danger.

"He deserves to have a ten-year-old life," King said. "Obsessing about every sport known to man, begging me to stay up late, losing brain cells on his tablet, hanging out with friends. Not this."

Scarlett moved to close the distance between them. Slower than she wanted to. Heat climbed into her neck as she pulled out the chair next to his and took a seat. A tremor shook through one hand as she reached out for his, enfolding it in her palms.

His skin was warmer—hot even—and rough with dryness from spending most of his days in the desert with a gun in his grip. But soft in other places, like the webbing between his fingers. She latched on, mostly for her own stability as this entire partnership threatened to fall apart. "Is there a chance the cartel knows Julien was there the night his mother was killed?"

"I asked the investigating detective to keep Julien out of all the reports because he was a minor." King stared down at his hand, as though he couldn't comprehend how he'd ended up here in this elementary school conference room with her when he was supposed to be out there looking for a connection between two past partners' murders. "You read the file. There's no mention of his name."

"Then we need to assume taking Julien is meant to be a warning to you." Air stalled in her chest as she internally braced for what came next. "Just as Adam Dunkeld was."

Surprise mixed with a hint of that anger as King leaned back in the chair. His hand went with him, leaving a streak of heat in her palms. "Muñoz. That son of a bitch. He's got to be the one behind this." Another shift wrecked the determination that flared in his eyes, gutting Scarlett in an instant. "Adam was missing for three days before he turned up dead at your doorstep."

And yet Eva Roday was murdered in her own home. There hadn't been an abduction. No grace period for law enforcement to play catch-up.

"King, if you're right about Muñoz being behind Eva's death, I think it's safe to say if the cartel learns Julien witnessed his mother's murder that night, he doesn't have that kind of time." She didn't want to put a countdown clock on this case, but they had no other choice.

"He's all I've got left, Scarlett. He's the only thing

that matters. All of this—working for the DEA, running that investigation on the side—I was doing it for him. To protect him."

The defensiveness she'd come to expect from King since he'd inserted himself into her life this morning wasn't there anymore. He'd been stripped of his armor by a ten-year-old, and there was nothing she could do about it. No security patch could fix this. She had no backup plan in place.

He brought his gaze to hers, the whites of his eyes reflecting the harsh fluorescent lights overhead. "And now they have him."

"We're going to get him back. Alive," she said. "I give you my word."

"Don't do that." The fire she'd witnessed behind all that devastation exploded. He shoved out of his chair, letting the wheels crash into the table leg. "Don't promise me something you have no intention of following through on, Scarlett. Because this is my son. This is my life, and if I lose him because your word isn't good enough, I will spend the rest of my life making you pay. You understand? So think very carefully about what you're promising me."

She pushed to her feet, meeting him on his level. "You asked about the scar across my stomach. You want to know how I got it? By keeping my word. I don't give it casually, King, and I don't give it to anyone who I don't believe deserves it. But once I do, I won't give up until I'm finished. Now, we can debate about the worth of my promises all day with examples and my résumé, but your son is out there. He doesn't have as much time as we need, and I'm one of the only people in this country who knows what we're dealing with. So are you going to trust me?"

He held his own, seemingly taking it all in one word at a time. "Yeah. I trust you."

"Good. The principal has queued the security footage taken during the time Julien was checked out. I suggest we start there." Pent-up energy flooded into the streak of scar tissue across her abdomen as she headed for the door. Most days she could pretend it didn't exist. That her closest friend hadn't tried to kill her while they'd been stationed overseas. Today wasn't one of those days. Scarlett wrenched open the door and stepped into the main office.

Formica-coated, two-tiered desks separated two administrators from the parents and students meant to stay on one side. Cabinets stacked high on one another behind each station and showed off motivational posters like the kind she used to hang in her room as a kid. An entire wall of glass gave school staff a view into the long corridors making up the industrial-carpeted school. Two doors provided access into the main school once entrants were allowed past the auto-locking doors.

Scarlett bypassed the officers taking statements from teachers and staff and headed down the hallway into the back of the main office. She clocked each and every camera installed throughout the space as she moved. Not enough. Not nearly enough to keep these tiny souls safe. Cutting to the principal's office at the very end of the hallway, she didn't bother to confirm whether King had kept up. "Principal Doleac. This is King Elsher. Julien's father."

"Yes, of course." A trim woman who looked as though

she lived off of long miles, few carbs and a tanning bed got up from behind her desk and offered her manicured hand. "I wanted to express how sorry I am about all of this, Mr. Elsher. We haven't had anything like this happen before. We will be working closely with Socorro and law enforcement to bring Julien home as quickly as possible. Anything you need, please don't hesitate to ask."

"You have the security footage of when my son was taken?" King didn't bother extending his own hand to shake.

The principal retracted into herself as she took a seat in front of an old monitor from the Stone Age. "Yes. I have it pulled up here. It's not the most sophisticated system, but as I said, we've never had anything like this happen before."

"Could you give us a few minutes?" Scarlett asked.

Hesitation deepened the lines around Doleac's eyes and mouth. Midforties, Scarlett would guess. Though she imagined the stress of the woman's job and the political pressure she handled on a day-to-day basis had added a few unkind years. "I'm sorry. I can't just leave you alone with the district's system. These computers contain students' private information and internal information about our teachers. I'm happy to navigate through whatever footage you need."

King set his badge on the principal's desk. "I'm not interested in teacher or student information, Principal Doleac. I'm here for my son. Anything we come across not pertaining to this case will remain confidential."

She studied the badge for a moment before climbing back onto impossibly high heels that accentuated how short Doleac really was. "Please let me know if I can be of any further assistance."

Scarlett slid into the principal's chair as the administrator made her way out of the office. A zing of anticipation crackled through her fingers as she scanned through the thumbnails of footage. "Their system could use an upgrade, but it seems simple enough to navigate. Let me pull up the camera and time Julien was checked out."

King shifted into her peripheral vision, then closer. Right up against her right side. Leveraging one hand against the desk and the other against the back of her chair, he pressed in. He pointed at the screen. "That's Julien."

The window expanded to the full width of the monitor and automatically started playing the footage. The angle looked as though it'd come from one of the cameras directly outside the office, recording students in the corridor leading up to the front of the building. The boy's face was pixelated, but there was no mistaking the similarity between him and the man beside her.

Scarlett studied King for a moment, taking in the softening of his jaw as he studied his son in the footage. "He has his backpack. So this must be after he was already called down to the office to get checked out. Which means we should be able to see who's waiting for him."

She sorted through the other frames recorded at the same time. And pulled up the image of a woman with her back to the camera. Thick curly hair pinned back away from the suspect's face, but there wasn't a good angle to get an ID. "She's avoiding the cameras. Let me see if I can follow them out to the parking lot."

Which meant whoever'd checked Julien out had been

in that school before. Had cased it. Knew the ins and outs. Most likely had a security blueprint or a map of the building. Julien's abduction hadn't been a one-off reaction to punish King for sticking his nose where it didn't belong. This was a coordinated effort.

"Do you recognize her?" Scarlett asked.

"Hard to tell without a shot of her face, but I've been through all the surveillance we have on Muñoz multiple times over. The only woman in his crew was killed a few months ago." King straightened, getting closer to the screen. "Wait. Look. Julien stops when he sees her."

He was right. Scarlett saw it then. The terror in the boy's face. A fawn response. She intensified the frame of Julien's face. "Like he's seen her before."

THERE WAS ONLY one reason for a ten-year-old boy to act like Julien had in that footage.

Fear.

A pressure King couldn't seem to get rid of followed him as he shoved through the elementary school's doors and out into the open. He scanned every car, every window from the houses facing the school. His son had been right here. Alone. Scared. Forced to follow the orders of a stranger or get hurt. King scrubbed a hand down his face. Damn it. He should've been here. Not chasing some dead end of a case he shouldn't have his nose in in the first place.

The school's exterior surveillance hadn't caught the vehicle Julien had been forced into, but King didn't need it. He knew who was behind this. And he knew exactly what he had to do to get his son back. He took his cell from his pocket.

"You're going to regret making that call." Scarlett's voice battled the loss and rage spiking through him. Which was impossible. He knew that, but there was something about her that argued with the natural man inside him that wanted to tear through this entire city to find Julien. And, hell, he wanted to give in to her. To feel some sense of peace for himself. For his family.

King let his thumb hesitate over the phone's screen. "What call is that?"

"The one where you call up the team you have sitting on Muñoz and give the order for them to breach the compound." Scarlett moved into his peripheral vision with far more grace than should be possible with all that gear she carried. Like she'd made it part of her over the years. Based on what she'd told him of her experience, he guessed that was true. "You're not in the right frame of mind to think about this logically. You're too close to it. The second your team crosses Muñoz's property line, you'll be declaring war with Sangre por Sangre."

"And you don't think kidnapping a DEA agent's son is an act of war?" His grip tightened around the phone as he turned to her. She was right. There was no logic behind this, but life wasn't always logical. It was the connections that made the difference between the ordinary and the meaningful, and the only one he cared about right now was Julien. "How about stabbing an agent through the chest?"

"Whoever did this is baiting you, King. They want you running off emotion instead of common sense. That's how they win, and if you make that call, you'll be playing directly into their hands," she said.

"Why?" That was the question. The one that'd been

constantly ticking at the back of mind after he'd gotten the call about Adam's murder this morning. It churned until he swore his blood started to boil. "First Adam, now Julien. My investigation into Muñoz didn't turn up anything significant. I have nothing. He's made sure to keep his hands off cartel business, so why make an example out of me? Why go after the people I care about?"

"I don't know." Scarlett stared out over the parking lot, seemingly memorizing the quickest exits and any vehicles that might get in her way. Like the good soldier she was supposed to be.

His gaze dropped to the hem of her T-shirt and the scar hiding beneath the fabric. She'd told him she'd gotten it by keeping her word. If that was true, she might be the only one who could help him now.

"According to our intel Muñoz is making a move for leadership," she said. "He wants the old regime out. You or your surveillance team must've stumbled across something that could put a stop to that. Killing your partner—abducting Julien—they're warnings."

The truth of it resonated through him, but no single piece of evidence came to mind. The pressure behind his sternum strangled the remaining air in his lungs. Helplessness threatened to erode the last of his strength. It took everything he had right then to stay on his feet as his mind replaced Eva's crime scene photos with ones featuring the boy he'd come to love more than life itself. "I'm all he has left, Scarlett. I promised I would take care of him. That as long as we were together, nothing could hurt him, and now…"

"I know." She stepped close to him. Tendrils of hair escaped the ponytail tied at the nape of her neck and tickled across his face. That simple focus conquered the downward spiral tearing through him. "I need you to listen to me. Sangre por Sangre doesn't play by the rules. They don't stick to MOs unless they're sending a message. There's no telling how much time Julien has, but if we can prove Muñoz was behind Eva and Adam's murders, we'll have the leverage to use against him. You know Muñoz's current operation better than anyone. Do you have any idea where the cartel might've held your partner during the three days he was missing?"

"I've been through Muñoz's holdings a hundred times." Addresses, bank accounts, phone records—all of it had been aboveboard to an outsider looking in. None of it useful. "He owns a couple car dealerships in town, a restaurant that's under investigation by the state health department and a couple McMansions outside the city."

Scarlett's face lit up. "The restaurant. The health department would've shut it down until Muñoz addressed the problems they found, right? No one would be allowed in or out, and restaurants usually come with those locking freezers. If Muñoz worked it right, he could've stashed Adam Dunkeld without anyone knowing."

He loved the way her brain worked. Electricity shot through him at the idea of their first real lead. King swiped through his phone and brought up the address, moving toward the SUV. "The restaurant is only a couple miles from here. I'll put in the request for the search warrant."

They moved as though they'd been partnered for more than a few hours. In step with each other. Scarlett rounded the SUV to the driver seat as King hauled himself into the other side. Both Dobermans paced back and forth across the cargo area. As though they sensed what was coming.

War.

He would go to war with the cartel for his son.

King submitted the warrant request up the DEA chain. He'd worked his own personal investigation into Muñoz up to this point, but stepping foot inside the restaurant without a warrant would throw anything they found into question. Or dismiss it altogether. And he couldn't take that risk. Not with Julien's life on the line.

The Dobermans stuck both of their heads over the center console with low groans.

"They don't look too pleased you left them in the car." King found himself leaning away from the duo. His instincts told him this breed could turn on him at any moment. One wrong move, and they'd turn him into their next meal.

"A lot of people hold grudges against Dobermans." Scarlett angled out of the elementary school's parking lot, bringing up the GPS on the SUV's navigation screen. "They believe the aggression is innate. That it can't be bred or trained out of them, so I try to keep the twins away from the general public. But in the year I've worked with Hans and Gruber since coming to Socorro, they've only grown more attached to me and the team, including the other K9s."

Attached enough to kill anything that threatened their handler? "I'll be sure to stay on your good side then."

Her laugh filled the cabin of the SUV and physically attacked the tension along his spine. Which shouldn't have been possible. Not when they were on their way to search a building where his partner could have been tortured and killed. Where Julien might be held now. But he was quickly learning what he saw of Scarlett wasn't exactly what he got. A security consultant for the country's most well-funded private military contractor would have to be controlled, perfectionistic and critical of everything and everyone she encountered, but at the same time there was a hint of softness in the way she spoke. A passion to help that he couldn't ignore.

"Only if you want to stay alive," she said.

They settled into a few minutes of silence as they got closer to the restaurant.

"This is it." Scarlett shoved the SUV into Park. She leaned over the console to get a better look through his window at the stucco building across the street.

Hints of her body soap—something like eucalyptus and lavender—filled his space and dove into his lungs. Soothing and exciting at the same time.

Unholstering her sidearm, she released the magazine and checked the ammunition before reassembling her weapon. Efficient. Quick. The woman knew her way around a gun. "Catalina's?" she asked.

"It's named after his wife." He'd never been here in person, but King felt as though he knew every inch of the place from the amount of surveillance he and his team had done over the past two months. He noted the pillars holding up the overhang protecting the double glass doors, intricate designs carved into the wood. Sharp corners and a flat roof complemented the look and feel of the surrounding buildings and homes with benches and plants funneling customers inside from the heat. "One entrance at the front, an exit at the back that leads into the alley between all these other buildings."

"How do you want to play this?" she asked.

King checked his phone. "We've got the search warrant." Unholstering his own weapon, he ensured his badge and credentials were visible to anyone who might want to intervene during their search. "That means we can knock on the front door."

"Great. I love Mexican food." She shouldered free of the vehicle and wrenched open the back door to let Hans and Gruber out. King followed suit. The Dobermans immediately rounded the SUV in playful leaps. *"Fuss."*

Each dog took to Scarlett's side as she holstered her weapon and headed for the restaurant's front door. "After you."

He'd waited a long time for this. King forced the knot in his gut out of his mind as he approached the building. No movement from the windows. A seal plastered over the double doors warned customers of the potential dangers of stepping foot inside, but he wasn't worried about E. coli or contracting food poisoning. King was here for his son. He pounded his fist against the thick wood. "Hernando Muñoz. DEA. We have a search warrant. Open up."

One minute. Two.

There was no answer from inside, and his heart rate notched higher.

"Let me help." Scarlett pulled a blade from one of her cargo pant pockets and slit the seal down the center. The Dobermans sniffed at the crack between the doors before she pulled at the handle. The doors parted with a frigid burst of air from inside. "Pretty sure these are supposed to be locked."

Warning flared in King's gut. He took to one side, Scarlett doing the same. "Go."

She stepped over the threshold, and the K9s followed close on her heels.

Swinging around the door, King swept his attention over a ghost town of chairs and tables. Dark walls and flooring made it hard to see without overhead lighting as they moved section by section. Blinds had been drawn to keep outsiders from looking in, but the edges lit up with bright sunlight that reflected off stacks of glasses.

He nodded toward a swinging door at the back of the building. "The kitchen."

"Right behind you," she said.

King took the lead. No matter what waited on the other side, he wanted to be the first through the door. Wanted Julien to see his father hadn't given up on him. Hinges protested as he shoved into the back room. Clean stainless steel glimmered as King hit the light switch to the right.

The K9s jogged ahead, spreading out. Before meeting in front of the oversize freezer doors.

"They've got something." Scarlett lowered her weapon but didn't move to put it away. Sidestepping to the freezer's handle, she glanced back at King. Silently waiting for his go-ahead.

He gave it.

She wrenched the door back, exposing what waited for them inside.

King held his breath as he moved into the too-small space but kept his distance so as not to disturb the blood patterns arcing across the floor and walls. Fresh. Recent. He lowered his weapon. "Adam was here."

Chapter Five

DNA didn't lie.

And right now it was telling them that Adam Dunkeld had suffered for a very long time before his killer or killers put him out of his misery.

Albuquerque PD's forensic unit moved in a chaotic dance. It'd taken less than an hour to confirm the blood's owner against the federal agent's file, and the entire DEA was on alert. A flash burst from the tech photographing every square inch of the refrigerator.

Scarlett wouldn't need to study these resulting photos. She couldn't unsee the patterns the blood spatter had made across the tile every time she closed her eyes. Couldn't help but wonder if routinely torturing people in the restaurant's fridge was what led to the county shutting the place down in the first place.

"I take it this is your first crime scene." King penetrated her peripheral vision as she watched the team move almost like a hive mind. Each knowing what to do and under orders to get it done.

The muscles down her back urged her to stand straighter, to be more prepared for the shot of heat darting through her. To be good enough to even stand next to an agent like King. "How can you tell?"

"You still have a little bit of throw-up on your vest." He nodded to her right shoulder, handing over a bottled water soaked in condensation. Sympathy softened the cut of his jaw and the lines around his eyes.

Scarlett took the bottle faster than she'd ever drawn her sidearm and chugged. Liquid leaked at the corners of her mouth as she attempted to wash the sick taste from her mouth, but there was no point.

"You're going to want to slow down." He settled into the worn cushioning of the other side of the booth, a thick wood table dividing them. "The faster you drink, the faster it comes up. Believe me."

"From experience?" she asked.

"Back when I was a rookie agent with the DEA, Sangre por Sangre was just getting its legs. They came in fast and hard by trying to knock out their competition. First time I set foot in a crime scene, the prosecutor assigned to the case had to convince the judge I wasn't a member of the cartel." His mouth hiked into a half smile that had the ability to freeze time if Scarlett allowed herself such small pleasures in life. "I left so much of my DNA all over that scene, the techs refused to work with me for a year. Any time Adam and I came up on a scene that required a crime scene unit, he had to be the one to put in the request or the techs would give us the runaround."

There was no way a knowledgeable, committed, responsible agent like King would ever contaminate or compromise a scene like that. "You're just trying to make me feel better."

"I'm really not." He took a slug of his own water. "Adam got the entire incident on video. Lucky for me, I get to experience that moment all over again every team Christmas party." The smile drained slowly, as though he just realized he wouldn't have to go through the embarrassment this year. "He was a good agent. A good friend. Deserved a hell of a lot better than I gave him."

She studied the pattern the photographer followed as he circled closer to the single chair with every compression of the shutter button. King was losing everyone he ever cared about. Methodically. "How long were you and Adam partnered together?"

"Since the beginning. We came up together. Recommended each other for promotions, knew each other better than anyone else. Right down to our allergies." He stared across the solid wood bar, through the propped-open kitchen door and into the refrigerator at the back. "I had Sunday dinner at his house every week with his wife and his kids, and I paid for lunch whenever we were out in the field. We'd spend hours driving across the state working cases in absolute silence. He was the kind of person who was fine not trying to fill every second with conversation but always knew when I needed a distraction. The fact people can do this kind of thing to each other never sat right with me, and Adam always knew what to say to make it a little more tolerable. Even right now, I'm expecting him to walk through those doors and make me feel better. We had a good thing going."

Her heart leaped at the opportunity to be that person for him. A replacement for his partner who could inject a small amount of good in the middle of so much bad. But being that source had nearly gotten her killed in the past. Her need to make up for all the terrible things she'd done would put her right back where she didn't want to be. And she'd worked too hard to take a step back now. "I'm sorry."

It was all she could think to say. And she meant it. With every cell in her body, she was sorry she couldn't make the hurt controlling him go away. But they weren't partners. They weren't friends. They were barely acquaintances. He was using her and Socorro to legitimize an off-the-books operation that'd led to the death of his partner and the kidnapping of his son. That was all she was. A resource.

Just as she'd been to the man who almost killed her.

But there was something about King that wanted to convince her she was more. In the way he thought about her needs in the middle of a scene where his partner and best friend had been murdered. The way he made every conversation lighter and pulled out the laugh she'd forgotten the sound of with sarcasm and banter. It'd been a long time since she'd felt this comfortable with a partner. And she almost wished she could hold on to that a little longer.

But she couldn't. This investigation would end. Sooner or later, they'd find Julien. King would go back to the DEA, and she'd return to Socorro. They couldn't make time stop. No matter how much she wanted to live in quiet moments like this. There was no point in trying.

Scarlett thumbed water beads off the bottle gripped between both hands. "What did Agent Roday have on the cartel?"

"What?" He cut his gaze to her.

"You said your partner was targeted to send you a

message, and from what I'm seeing here, I'm inclined to believe Sangre por Sangre was using Adam to get to you or at least to learn what you had on them." Her brain frantically scrambled to connect the dots. When a piece of circuitry failed in the security system she'd hardwired into Socorro's headquarters, the whole system was compromised. It was her job to make sure her team was safe. She couldn't do that with gaping holes. "But Julien's mother was killed two months ago. You hadn't spoken in years. You didn't even know about your son, and it was her murder that triggered your investigation into Muñoz. There must've been a reason the cartel considered her a threat."

"I reached out to the supervisory special agent over Eva's unit a couple days after the social worker brought me Julien." King directed his attention back to the officers working the scene, taking any prints that might've been left behind and marking areas safe to walk through the restaurant. "He claimed whatever Eva was working on before she died was above my pay grade. Classified. He couldn't or wouldn't tell me if the job was what got her killed, but I know for a fact Eva had looked into Muñoz in the past."

"How can you be so sure?" she asked.

"That case we worked together, the one before we…"

The idea of him and the mother of his child together shouldn't hit her nervous system as hard as it did.

King leveraged one arm against the shiny, lacquered table. "The DEA asked her to consult on a device we uncovered during one of our operations. We'd gotten intel from an informant that Sangre por Sangre and the head of the Marquez cartel out of Mexico were meeting in a warehouse outside the city. But by the time my team got there, we were just recovering pieces of the device after it did its job tearing through a good chunk of the Marquez cartel. Turned out, Sangre por Sangre was on a mission to consolidate power."

"You said Adam had been with you from the beginning," she said. "Was he there for that operation?"

"Of course. We…" King sat up a bit straighter. "We've been partners for over ten years. That was one of the first assignments we took on together."

The answer was right there in front of them. A time and place where both victims had come together against the Sangre por Sangre cartel. A connection. The first real lead they'd had so far. "Then they knew each other, at least peripherally. Is there any chance Agent Dunkeld and Agent Roday have been in contact since that operation?"

King scrubbed a hand down his face. "I don't know. Adam never said anything if he was, and police didn't find anything in Eva's phone records or emails to come to that conclusion."

There was another explanation. Because the odds of two federal agents being stabbed to death in the span of two months—both of which landed in King's orbit—were too great to ignore. "Unless your partner didn't want you to know."

"What are you saying?" He turned that internal intensity that could start a wild fire given enough space on her, and Scarlett's defenses spiked. He shoved free of the booth and circled until he cut off her view of his face. "You think Adam and Eva were working on something together? There's no way. He was my partner. We told each other everything, and he was a shit liar. Did everything by the book. I would've known if he was keeping something from me."

"What if he couldn't tell you?" Scarlett got to her feet, closing the distance between them. "Think about it. If Eva was investigating Sangre por Sangre and Muñoz after all these years, she would've needed a contact in the DEA. Someone who was there during that operation, but she couldn't come to you. Not without telling you about Julien, and she obviously didn't want that seeing as how she kept his existence a secret from you for ten years. So is it possible she reached out to Adam to get what she needed?"

His shoulders slowly relaxed away from his ears as King faced her. "It's possible, but I don't see how going through a ten-year-old operation gets her Muñoz or helps bring my son home now."

Scarlett latched on to his forearm as the potential for answers heated through her. "Then let's go find out."

HE COULD STILL feel her.

That single touch that had somehow released the pressure valve behind his sternum.

The scene at the restaurant would take hours, if not days, to process. Time he and Scarlett didn't have. Because if she was right, if a decade-old DEA operation was the reason Adam and Eva had been killed all these years later, and was why his son had been taken, they couldn't wait for answers.

But he hadn't wanted to find them here.

"You sure you want to start here?" Scarlett met him

at the end of the driveway as Hans and Gruber sniffed their way down the sidewalk.

It probably didn't seem like much from her end, but having her here meant something. It meant she was going to keep her word, that in a world where he couldn't even trust the man he'd partnered with all these years, she was going to come through.

"I've been putting it off long enough." Well-maintained bushes hid the initial view of the house he'd been to every morning for the past ten years. It wasn't anything spectacular, but the clean rockscaping punctuated with bright purple cactus flowers told him the place was loved.

King hiked up the oil-spotted driveway toward the two-car garage hiding the view of the front door. A large bay window on the other side provided the homeowner with a view that guaranteed she saw them coming, and nervous energy shocked through him.

It wasn't every day you had to tell your partner's wife he wasn't coming home.

Hinges protested from the metal screen installed over the front door before he had a chance to ring the doorbell. The woman folding her arms over her chest in the doorframe barely had anything left to grab on to. She wasn't taking care of herself, that much was clear in the thinness of her skin and the oil overtaking her blond hair. She was close to six months pregnant, but from her current size, he might've assumed three. Four max. She'd pulled it back into a ponytail. He wasn't sure he'd ever seen her without those signature waves, a couple layers of makeup or the leggings she liked to wear despite the heat.

No echoes of kids yelling or something being thrown down the hallway after Adam had told them for the thousandth time their mother was going to kill them for playing soccer in the house.

King pulled up short at the base of the walkway and just…stopped. Too heavy to get the words out. He hadn't wanted this. Ever. He didn't want to be the one standing here. In his mind, he always pictured it the other way around. Adam followed the book. Never took a risk unless King was the one to push him. King should've been the one the cartel had dragged into that refrigerator. Not his partner.

Warmth prickled at his arm where Scarlett had touched him, as though she were still touching him. Giving him the courage he needed right then. "Hi, Jen."

"He's dead, isn't he?" Chipped fingernails dug into Jen's arms as she ducked her chin to her chest, and King's entire world threatened to split open.

"Yeah. Adam's dead." There wasn't any more to say. Nothing he could do to take on her pain, even for just a few seconds. He was powerless in this moment, and he hated the feeling with every fiber of his being. King crossed the distance to the front door, prying his partner's wife away from the doorframe and into his arms. "I'm so sorry. I wasn't there. I couldn't protect him."

Jen pressed her face into his chest. Sobs tremored through her body until all he heard was great big gasps for breath. Digging those usually manicured nails into his arms, she cried until there was nothing left.

King didn't know how long they stood there with Scarlett watching. He didn't care. Because he owed this to Jen. Owed Adam.

"Tell me how. How did this happen?" she asked.

"The cartel." It was all he would give her. His partner's family deserved to remember him as he was. Not as the corpse he'd ended up.

Life bled into Jen's face and replaced the paleness there. She shoved at him with one hand, though she didn't come close to knocking him off balance. "You came into my home every day, King. I welcomed you at our breakfast table. I let you near my children because you promised. You promised me every morning before you and Adam left that you would back him up."

She shoved him again. This time with both palms, and King took a big step back as she advanced. The metal screen door snapped closed.

"Why weren't you there, King? Why weren't you the one…" Another wave of emotion cut her short as she brought her hands to her face. Jen doubled over as her strength failed.

"I wanted to be." And he had. A thousand times over in the hours since he'd gotten the call about his partner. He'd wanted to be the one on the slab. To save Jen and the kids from the black well of grief. But that wasn't how life had played out. King raised his gaze to Scarlett. She was good at fixing things, but she couldn't fix this. No matter how much he wanted her to. "Jen, I need to know. Was Adam working on anything off the books? Did he say anything about an operation the DEA ran ten years ago or mention the name Eva Roday in the past few days?"

The sobs quieted to a low moan. Jen pushed back the tendrils of hair that escaped her crude ponytail. The fire that'd held Adam captive for years exploded in her eyes. She straightened, facing off with him as the roller coaster of pain and loss vanished.

"You son of a bitch. Really? You tell me Adam isn't coming home, that the cartel killed him, and you're asking me if there's anything my husband said about a case he was working five seconds later." She poked a finger into his chest. "You're always chasing answers, King, but you know what the sad thing is? You're never going to be happy with what you've got. Adam felt bad for you, you know. Said this job was all you had, even after you learned about Julien. That's why he thought it was so important to stay your partner and turn down all those promotions that came his way. And he was right. You're always going to be looking for that next lead. Letting the things that matter pass you by."

The words stabbed through him, one at a time, until King couldn't take his next breath.

Scarlett took a step forward, and he knew right then she would always be the one to take that first step. Into the fight, to stand up for those who couldn't stand up for themselves. It was just the kind of person she was, and he admired the hell out of that. "Hey, that's—"

He held Scarlett off as the pull of something desperate and illogical took control. Jen was right. He'd built his entire life around this job. It'd gotten him through, given him purpose. It'd kept him focused when he suddenly found himself taking care of a kid who wouldn't talk to him and missing the woman he'd let slip through his fingers. But it wasn't what was driving him now. "They took my son, Jen."

Shock stole the anger in Jen's expression. Her finger drifted from his chest as she lost the will to keep him in his place. She blinked those big doe eyes filled with tears. "What?"

"They took Julien." And King lost the will to keep years of classified intel, secrets and emotions to himself as the truth bled into existence. "I know I failed you. I know there's nothing I can do to bring Adam home, and you're more than welcome to hate me for the rest of your life, if that's what you need to do. But there is a little boy out there in the hands of the very people who murdered your husband. And he's scared, Jen. He doesn't know what's going to happen to him or if anyone's coming for him. Help me get to him. Please."

One second. Two.

Jen stared at him, and hell, King didn't know what she saw. He just hoped it was enough. "Adam never said anything about his cases. I didn't want to know after…" She didn't have to finish that sentence. He knew about her family, about how she was raised by an addict who frequently beat her and her brother when her stepdad was coming down from a high. It was a life she worked hard to leave behind. "But I knew he was working on something that wasn't for the DEA. I have a strict rule about bringing work home from the field, and he never broke that rule. But I caught him two weeks ago in the middle of the night. In his office. He was unscrewing the cover on the air return vent and putting something inside."

Anticipation shot through him. "Did you see what it was?"

"No. And I didn't ask." Jen leveled that gaze at him, a hardness taking over that he'd only ever seen when Adam and the kids were in trouble. It only lasted a moment before the grief moved back in. She folded in on herself all over again, and right then, Jen suddenly seemed so much smaller than he remembered.

Adam's life insurance would cover hers and the kids' cost of living, most likely pay off this house, but there were some things money couldn't take on, and King would be the one to step up. To make sure they got through this.

"But I haven't touched anything in there since he went missing," Jen said. "I figured…he would want it to stay as he left in when he came home. And if not, then the DEA might need to go through it first."

She moved aside, giving him and Scarlett a clear shot to the front door. "Find the bastards who did this and get your son back, King. Make them wish they hadn't come after your family."

"I intend to." King didn't wait as he pried the metal screen door open and crossed the threshold, Scarlett and her Dobermans close behind.

The front door deposited them straight into a tidy living room with worn carpet and oversize leather couches. The dining room that'd hosted a thousand family breakfasts every morning King had showed up to collect his partner stared back at him with a grudge. There wouldn't be any more breakfasts at that table. Not for him.

"The office is this way." He moved down the hall on instinct until they found the room they were looking for. The house wasn't all that big, but there were enough rooms to give the kids their own and provide an office for Adam with a view out the back window.

Hesitation gripped the small muscles in the bottom of King's feet as he set eyes on the air return vent Jen had mentioned. Three steps. That was all it took to set himself beneath it. The screws popped out easier than he expected, and King jammed his hand into the vent.

Something was stuffed inside the return.

"What is it?" Scarlett held on to each of the dogs' collars as he brought down a manila file folder.

"Some kind of file. I've never seen it before." King flipped open the cover. And froze at the notepaper clipped inside the front cover.

Scarlett moved in to get a better look, raising her gaze to his. She took the folder from him and scanned through his partner's handwritten notes. "Looks like Adam was running his own off-the-books investigation into the cartel. With Eva Roday, from what I can see of these notes."

"Yeah." A million thoughts were going through his head, but King only had attention for one. He pointed to a section of notes Adam had circled over and over. "And figured out Sangre por Sangre is far more dangerous than we gave them credit for."

Chapter Six

It was all there.

Scarlett had read the file they'd recovered from Adam's office so many times the words were starting to blur together. Every detail accounted for. Every move Muñoz had made over the past decade. It all made sense.

Sangre por Sangre hadn't just started consolidating power by taking out the heads of the other cartels during that DEA operation ten years ago. They'd been absorbing the orphaned soldiers left behind. And accepting funds from an outside source.

Overseas funds.

The kind that never ran out. The kind that came from organizations that had outlived the fall of governments and were impossible to dismantle because of their sheer size. Sangre por Sangre had always been in the drug business, but the partnership that Agents Dunkeld and Roday theorized was slowly taking place revealed something so much worse.

The drugs confiscated at the borders every day were a mere fraction of what actually got through. Cartels were willing to take the risk, knowing the payoff was worth a small sacrifice of product, but with this? Sangre por

Sangre would have unfettered access. Humans. Drugs. Weapons. There was no limit if this intel was right.

"Ten years of operations." King pressed his thumb and index finger into his eyes. He checked his phone again. She'd lost count of how many times, but there was no word about Julien. The tension in his shoulders relayed nothing but concern and impatience. Albuquerque PD had nothing. "Neither of them said a word."

She and King had been at this for an hour, trying to absorb as much of Adam's notes as possible. The sun had dipped behind the half-moon ring of mountains to the west. All of this… It was too much for any one person. Or maybe the information was meant to be shared by a team. Designed to ensure one person didn't have to take it all on themselves.

Scarlett closed the file on her lap. Sweat built along the collar of her shirt as Hans and Gruber kicked in their sleep from the corner of the room.

Turned out the vent in this office wasn't actually functional for anything other than a poor man's safe. Adam Dunkeld purposefully put himself in misery every time he sat down at this desk to work the investigation. As though he were punishing himself.

But he had company every single time. Scarlett's gaze turned to the family photo facing off with her from the corner of the desk. Of smiling faces and happier times. The chair protested as she leaned forward. Her joints screamed for release. "I imagine Eva wanted it that way. In case something happened to her. That way Julien had somewhere to go. Somewhere he'd be safe."

"Maybe you're right." King tossed his section of the file onto the desk and pushed to stand. "Doesn't make it any easier to swallow, though. Because now my son is right where Eva didn't want him, and there's not a damn thing I can do to help him."

Not until they figured out Muñoz's involvement in all this. Adam Dunkeld and Eva Roday had stumbled onto something Socorro hadn't even considered possible for the enemy they'd been fighting, but the intel fit. The increase in soldiers, the upgrade in weapons and armored vehicles. The escalation in violence, abductions and raids. Sangre por Sangre wasn't the same small-time cartel Socorro had been contracted to dismantle. This was a new threat altogether. One they didn't know.

"You haven't heard anything?" Scarlett asked.

"No. No ransom call. No request for money." King did that thing where he scrubbed a hand down his face before checking his phone. "Which means they're not interested in negotiating."

He didn't need to finish that sentence. It was already burned into the front of her mind. Julien's abductors weren't interested in negotiating because they had no intention of letting the ten-year-old come home alive. It'd taken all her persuasive powers to get him to slow down enough to uncover some kind of lead from these files. But was it enough?

Scarlett couldn't take the thought of watching King lose someone else. This man who'd already sacrificed so much for the innocent lives he protected from the cartel, who'd already lost everything and everyone. She needed to contact Socorro and hand over the intel they'd uncovered. Ivy had to know what they were up against. Every second Sangre por Sangre was connected to whoever was funding them overseas, the less chance she and her team had of winning this war.

But there was something she had to do first. Something only she could fix. "What if we don't wait for Julien's kidnappers to contact you? What if we go get Julien ourselves?"

A mirrored ache to do *something* carved into King's expression. "We don't have proof Lieutenant Muñoz is behind my son's abduction. If we go in there without a solid lead, we could be putting Julien in more danger."

"You're right. But what if we find him?" And Scarlett wanted to find that boy. More than anything. For King. "We might not have hard evidence, but there's enough in these files to support a real DEA investigation into Muñoz. And it all started with that operation ten years ago. That can't be a coincidence. What if your suspicion hasn't been for nothing? What if Muñoz is at the center of all of this? That he had Eva Roday and your partner killed. That he's the one who sent his crew after Julien."

King's left hand fisted and released. "I can't walk into DEA headquarters with a theory and authorize a raid team, even with Adam's proof that there's something more going on inside the cartel. And I know Ivy Bardot well enough to know she's going to want solid evidence that Sangre por Sangre has my son before she signs off on any operation Socorro will be linked to." His shoulders hiked on a deep inhale. "So how would we do this?"

Scarlett dragged out a photo from a decade's worth of surveillance. "We start here. As for backup, you have me and the twins. That's all you'll need."

"You certainly think highly of yourself, don't you?" King studied the photo of a warehouse. Ten years ago,

the DEA had found the *hefe* of the Marquez cartel hand-
less with a bullet between his eyes. This was where it
had all started for Adam Dunkeld and Eva Roday. Investigators had needed to scrape the body of the former
Marquez cartel leader off the floor to collect his remains
that day, and King had been there. Was everything that'd
happened since then punishment?

"With good reason." Scarlett tapped the photo.

"What makes you think Muñoz stashed Julien here?"
he asked.

"Because he knows you were there that day during
the DEA operation." Her brain had settled into strategy
mode. Where she took apart the problem in front of
her and figured out a way to go around it. Or through
it. It was one of the skills her instructors and the army
had taken advantage of more often than not. "Muñoz is
smart. He's managed to gather support for overthrowing
the head of Sangre por Sangre while keeping himself
alive these past few months. He doesn't leave anything
to chance, because one wrong move could take him out.
Which means he'll have studied you. Your habits, rou-
tines, the people you surround yourself with. He'll want
to know everything about you, including your operation
history, which cases you seem to take a particular inter-
est in, how you approach an investigation. He would've
known Adam was your partner and started looking into
him, too."

"Doesn't explain why Adam's body was dropped outside Socorro headquarters. But you think he's been watching me?" His voice hitched on that last word. "Watching
Julien?"

"And anyone else in your life. It's what I would do."

The plan was already taking shape in her mind. Where she would be, how she'd breach. All from a single photo. Though a decade-old surveillance picture wasn't enough to make a move on. She needed up-to-date intel. "But I'd bet Muñoz's fascination with you started when he suspected Eva Roday was closing in. She most likely led the cartel to Adam, then to you."

"And now Julien." King seemed to break free of the stiffness in his body. "Do you think… Do you think they know Julien was there the night Eva was killed? That he saw the person who killed his mother?"

Scarlett lost her train of thought, taken aback by his concern for a little boy he hadn't even known existed up until a couple months ago. And remembering the utter look of sheer terror on Julien's face from that surveillance footage. King had stepped into the role of father despite not knowing how the hell to take care of anyone but himself, and it looked good on him. All that intensity, all that defensiveness and lack of trust he applied to saving lives through his work was nothing compared to the obvious love burning through him. That was what would bring his son back now. "No. I don't think the cartel is aware Julien was there that night. If they were, he would already be dead."

There would be nothing left for them to save.

"Okay. What now?" He nodded, seemingly convincing himself this was the best course of action, that at the end of this, he'd have his son back. No matter the consequences.

She gathered the file together in one pile and whistled low to call the Dobermans from sleep. Each snapped to attention and got to their feet. "We need to get eyes on the warehouse. Photos help, but they don't tell me everything I need to know."

"All right. Let me tell Jen we're leaving." King stepped free of the hot, too-small office and headed down the lengthy hall to the back of the house.

Investigation file in hand, Scarlett caught sight of the interaction that seemed to stretch mere seconds into full minutes. Of King's hand on the widow's arm, of how he'd lowered his voice as another sob shook through the woman.

A knot twisted in Scarlett's stomach, reminding her of a time when she'd needed someone like King there when her entire world had fallen apart. But she'd had no one. Too ashamed to tell her parents the truth, outcast by the rest of her unit. Dishonorably discharged with nothing and no one to fall back on. If it hadn't been for Granger Moraise and Ivy Bardot, Scarlett would hate to think of where she'd have ended up. Who would've come for her if she hadn't had Socorro's protection.

Her throat dried as King secured his partner's wife in his arms, and Scarlett didn't have the guts to watch anymore. Jealousy had the ability to do that. To take a heartfelt moment and twist it into something ugly and lacking, and she hated herself for it. That no one had been there to do the same for her when the person she'd cared about the most had betrayed her and everything he'd believed in.

Didn't matter. Rescuing a ten-year-old boy from his abductors mattered. It was the *only* thing that mattered, and the only way Scarlett could redeem herself.

King broke away from the grieving widow and

headed toward her. "I'm ready. Just tell me what you need me to do."

There was a level of trust in that statement. It dug beneath the shame and guilt of her past life and burrowed deep in her chest, annihilating any lingering layer of jealousy and resentment for not getting the care she deserved all those months ago. King was willing to give up the ego built over years of DEA operations for the slightest chance of recovering his son.

She had a plan. They could do this as long as they worked together. Scarlett headed for the door. "Have you ever handled C-4 before?"

HE HADN'T EVER planned on coming back here.

Old yellow external spotlights peppered the building and chased back the closing darkness. Didn't help. No matter what Scarlett had planned for them to get inside, they would be working in the dark. And King hoped like hell he'd be enough to get Julien through what came next.

"Place is registered under a shell company. It'll take a while to untangle who really owns it, but that's not the purpose of today's field trip." Scarlett swiped her finger across the tablet, casting a white-blue glow across her face and chest from the driver seat. "Doesn't look like it has any active permits. At least not from what I can see, which means there's a chance we could be walking into an empty building. It's got a great security system, though."

He ran his gaze over the harsh corners and along the rooftop. No cameras. "How can you tell?"

"The keypads on the doors." She nodded through the

windshield to the nearest side door, an outline that nearly
bled into the rest of the building. "That brand is one of
two Socorro installs for our clients. I've already checked.
We weren't the ones who put it in, but no one installs
that kind of system on an empty building. They're trying to keep people out for a good reason. Oh, they have
Wi-Fi. That helps."

"Or they're trying to keep somebody in." The words
didn't quite make it across the center console. King
memorized the outlines of rows and rows of orange
cable he usually saw on the side of the road during the
summer lined up behind the warehouse. Construction
crews always seemed to be closing lanes to lay it down
somewhere, but it was hard to imagine Sangre por Sangre creating a utility business and benefiting the infra-
structure of the state they were trying to take control
of. Which could mean they were in the wrong place.

Dead flat landscape stretched out into a sea of noth-
ingness. The other warehouses in the area had gone dark
a long time ago. Years of threats and instability in the
area had driven out a good chunk of businesses as the
cartel grew. If King remembered right, there was a dried-
up canal just on the other side of the single construction
trailer to the right.

The warehouse itself wasn't anything special—a rectangle with gray-white panels for walls. The bright blue
rolltop door stood out, though. Julien's favorite color of
the week. His son could be behind that door. Scared.
Calling for help and not getting a single answer back.
The thought heated King's palms. "Are we doing this
or what?"

"I've piggybacked off their W-Fi and accessed the

security system." Scarlett's fingers moved across the screen as though she were playing the most complicated piano concerto. Pure magic. "I can take it down from here."

King tried to get a good look at her tablet screen, seeing nothing but a mess of code he didn't understand. "Wait. You can do that?"

"Ride with me long enough, and you'll see that's not the only thing I can do." Scarlett reached into the back seat, rousing the Dobermans as she pulled a heavy Kevlar vest forward. One for her, then one for him. "We have about ten minutes before the security company realizes the system isn't reporting back and brings the system back online. You ready?"

He slipped his head through the opening in the vest and strapped it tight. Nervous energy prickled at the back of his neck, almost as if in warning, but there was no way in hell King was going to turn around now. Not with the possibility his son was in there. "Let's do this."

They shouldered out of the vehicle at the same time, keeping low and to the shadows. Hans's and Gruber's nails tapped against the asphalt but not loud enough to illicit a security response. King slid through the long line of cement parking space barriers. No vehicles in the lot, and half of the pine tree rooted at the corner of the building had succumbed to dry rot. They should have a straight shot inside, but his gut was telling him it wouldn't be that easy.

It never was with Sangre por Sangre.

Unholstering his sidearm, King crossed the crumbling parking lot to where the tree provided cover. And waited. His breath lodged in his throat. The night was thick with heat, and he couldn't swallow past the doubt. This didn't feel right. Of all the raids he'd executed over the years, this one felt uncomfortable.

King didn't have time to dig into that now. Julien needed him.

He scanned the surrounding desert as Scarlett reached for the pocket door nearest their location. Ten minutes wasn't enough time. Not for a place this size, but he'd do whatever it took to recover his son before those seconds ran out. He gave the okay to breach as he had a dozen times before.

Scarlett wrenched the door back on its hinges and stepped into the blackness waiting to consume them, weapon raised. The Dobermans followed without hesitation. Just before King was swallowed by a vast emptiness on the other side.

His heart rate doubled, thudding hard behind his ears as his senses tried to make up for the complete lack of stimulus. He pressed his feet down harder into the cement floor. He was grounded. As for everything else, he was at a loss.

A click registered in his ears, and a beam cut across the floor in front of him. Holding up one hand, he tried to block the onslaught of light, but it was no use. His senses couldn't adapt that fast.

"You look like you've seen a ghost." Scarlett directed the beam toward the floor and the K9s at her feet. "Come on. We don't have much time before the security company alerts whoever owns this place we're here."

He followed Scarlett's outline. Both hands gripped around his weapon, he took in as much as their limited light source provided.

The layout had changed in the last ten years. Now it was designed as a completely open space with exposed girders stretching across the ceiling. Some kind of inventory created a maze with pallets of crates stacked four or five high. Each box sported red-and-yellow stripes along one side, as if Scarlett and King had been thrown into some kind of messed-up circus he didn't want to get lost in. Two forklifts were wedged under pallets ahead. But it was the unending rows of product that had him picking up the pace.

There was no evidence a bomb had gone off in here ten years ago that'd required the ATF to consult. No sign of the past infiltrating into the present. It was as though that operation had never happened, and yet Adam and Eva couldn't seem to let this place go during their investigation into the cartel.

It didn't matter. King was here for one reason. "They wouldn't leave Julien out in the open. There's got to be offices or something around here."

"Follow me." Scarlett pressed forward with all that confidence King wished he could siphon for himself. She was every bit the military operator she was supposed to be, and there wasn't a single cell in his body that wasn't grateful for her at a time like this. A time when his training had seemingly gone out the window in search of the only person he had left.

She carved a path to the right, weapon held high as though the weight wasn't getting to her like it was to him, and heel-toed it forward like she'd already memorized the layout. Which, she probably had. They passed a steel support running straight up to the ceiling with another row of the red-and-yellow-striped boxes to his left, and that obsessed part of himself that'd pushed him from case to case all these years King prodded him from inside.

He slowed, trying to keep an eye on Scarlett and the Dobermans as he studied the nearest box.

"What are you doing?" The flashlight beam landed at his feet. Scarlett retraced her steps to him. "We have to keep moving. We have about two minutes before the security system pings."

"The photos in Adam's file. He and Eva were watching this place." King holstered his weapon, punctuated by one of the Doberman's low groans. He wasn't sure which. "I need to know why my partner and Julien's mother were killed. I need to know what the cartel is trying to hide."

He pulled a switchblade from his pocket and sliced the packing tape straight down the middle. Grabbing on to Scarlett's wrist, he forced her to angle the flashlight inside.

Packing peanuts stuck to the liner of the box and threatened to go everywhere with one wrong move. He drove his hand inside and felt around.

Then hit something solid. He grabbed on to it, even as he felt every second slipping through their fingers, and pulled the object free. Big blue eyes stared back at him.

A baby doll—heavier than he thought it should be—closed its eyes the farther he leaned it back. Her purple pajamas were pristine with yellow-and-white stripes, but there was something wrong about the angle of her head. King gripped the doll's head with one hand and her body with the other and pulled.

The jolt dislodged hundreds of light blue pills from inside.

"Holy hell." Scarlett followed the spill, crouching to get a better look. "These are fentanyl tabs. Enough to kill a herd of elephants."

There weren't many people outside of the DEA who could identify a pill just by the look and color of it. He was impressed.

Cutting the flashlight back to the box, Scarlett shoved to stand and sank her hand back into the box. She pulled out nine more dolls before turning the beam out into the rest of the warehouse. "Ten dolls per box."

King followed her line of thinking. "In a warehouse packed with boxes. Shit. There has to be enough to here to OD fifty million people."

"Sangre por Sangre has never dealt in fentanyl before." There was something off in her voice. A combination of shock and anger and heaviness they didn't have time to sit with. "Do you think this has something to do with the overseas resources Agents Dunkeld and Roday uncovered?"

"I don't know." He pulled a small rectangular bag from his back pocket—a necessity for DEA agents—and bagged a few of the pills as evidence.

A trio of beeps echoed through the warehouse and singed every nerve King owned. "What the hell was that?"

"The security system. It's back online." Scarlett cast the flashlight beam down the row of boxes that didn't seem to have an end. "They know we're here."

Chapter Seven

The lights flared to life and blinded her for a split second.

The first bullet barely missed Scarlett's head.

The box at her left hit the floor from the impact and scattered ten baby dolls at her feet. Big wide eyes stared up at her. Hans and Gruber growled in unison, and every muscle down Scarlett's back hardened in battle-ready defense. A wash of adrenaline had her reaching for King. "Get down!"

She used her body weight to pull him to the floor, dragging him beneath her. The second bullet cut through the maze of boxes and pinged off the support column less than two feet from her. Right where he would've been standing.

"You just can't help yourself, can you?" King's breath mixed with hers. "Underneath me in the morgue, on top of me here. You're insatiable."

"Glad to know where your head is at." She rolled to her right. They couldn't stay here. Not without catching the next bullet. "The blueprints of this place outlined an emergency exit on the north side of the building. I can get you there, but I need you to do everything I say. Understand?"

Hans and Gruber were at the ready. Just waiting for her to give the command, but Scarlett wasn't interested in facing off with the cartel in a last stand to the death. Her job was to get them all out alive.

"I'm not leaving." King punctuated the three words by cokcing a round into the barrel of his sidearm. "I need to know if Julien is here."

"You don't get it, do you?" Low shouts echoed through the maze of aisles and stacks. Four distinct voices so far. Most likely more. The potential carved through her, hiking her heart rate higher until it was all she could hear. "We're in enemy territory. Outnumbered and outmanned. And the only way we're leaving this warehouse alive is if we go right now. Winding up dead doesn't help anyone, King."

"I'm not leaving without my son." An energy Scarlett used to recognize in herself lit up his eyes. Determination. Desperation. The line between the two was thinner than most people thought. He maneuvered into a crouch, weapon in hand, and chanced standing a bit taller to gauge the situation. "Where are the offices?"

"You don't have to do this." She hated the words coming out of her mouth. Hated the tension combing through her, the dryness at the back of her throat. She'd trained on blood-soaked battlefields and handled security that saved thousands of lives over the course of her military career. But she didn't want to do this.

Scarlett leveraged her heels into the cement floor, pressing her back against the nearest stack of boxes. She couldn't think. Couldn't get herself to move. What the hell was happening? "We have an evidence bag of pills.

We can take what we know to the DEA and Socorro. We don't have to do this alone."

"Where are they, Scarlett?" His tone shut down any chance of changing his mind. Locking that hard gaze on her, King shook his head. "You know what? I don't have time for this. I'll find the offices myself."

He kept low as he cut down the nearest aisle.

"Wait." The sinking feeling in her stomach wouldn't let up. She reached after King but only met thin air. It wasn't supposed to be like this. They were a team. But she couldn't make herself move. Even as those low shouts got closer.

He vanished into another row, out of sight.

Leaving her to fight alone.

Hans practically vibrated from her next growl. Louder. A warning.

"Move, damn it." Scarlett knocked her head back into a box in hopes of resetting her brain. She couldn't stay here. Sliding one hand farther out, she focused everything she had on going after King. He was going to get himself killed. Too blind to protect himself with only the slightest chance of protecting his son.

Movement registered off to her right at the head of the aisle. Gruber barked a split second before Scarlett's instincts brought the weapon up. She squeezed her finger around the trigger. A spray of bullets shot into the ceiling as the gunman fell backward.

Her position was compromised.

"Okay." She could do this. She had to do this. And she had to do it now. Scarlett shoved to her feet and took that initial step in King's wake. This was what she was trained for. What she was good at. She wasn't going to let him do it alone. Her feet felt heavier than they should have as she whistled for Hans and Gruber to follow. "I'm coming."

Another burst of gunfire exploded from somewhere else in the warehouse. Her entire nervous system homed on that sound. She picked up the pace. "King."

Return fire—deeper in tone—cut through the chaos. He was still alive. She could still make this right between them. Scarlett slowed at the end of the aisle.

A fist rocketed into her face.

Lightning struck behind her eyes. She fell back. Pain launched into her elbows as she failed to cushion her impact.

Hans and Gruber didn't wait for an order, launching forward. The attacker's scream bounced off the warehouse's metal walls as each Doberman took a piece of the cartel soldier for themselves. Stumbling to her feet, Scarlett struggled to breathe through the blood cascading down her face. Her nose was broken. *"Hier."* Come.

The twins released their death hold on the soldier and promptly fell back in line at Scarlett's feet. Blood spread over the gunman's arms and stained his shirt. The sight of which held her hostage for far too long. She'd signed on with Socorro to do good. This...wasn't it.

Groans escaped up his throat. Still alive. Swiping the back of her hand beneath her nose, she stood over him, weapon ready to finish the job. "How many of you are there?"

Cradling his arms to his chest, he spat at her boot. "You don't have a chance."

Scarlett was ready to leave him there. Ready to make him suffer, but she couldn't have him following after her. She slammed the butt of her pistol against his head, knocking him unconscious. "I already know that."

She moved slower than she wanted to. The click of Hans's and Gruber's nails kept her focused. In the present. On alert. Dead silence seemed to settle through the warehouse and vaulted her unease through the roof.

Something was wrong.

The return fire she'd identified from King's weapon had gone quiet. Did that mean...? No. She couldn't think like that. Couldn't let herself get distracted. Find King. Get him out. That was all that mattered. "Please still be alive."

A howl pierced through her ears.

Every cell in Scarlett's body fired in defense as she turned. Hans was down. Unmoving on the cement. *No. No, no, no, no.*

Gruber launched at the threat coming from ahead. They were surrounded, being pulled in two different directions. Gruber took down his target as strong arms locked around Scarlett's neck from behind. Oxygen locked in her throat and chased back that sinking feeling that'd taken control.

"I was hoping I would be the one to get my hands on you." The man at her back pulled her into his chest, his grating voice at her ear. "Scarlett Beam. Socorro's most feared operative. Let's see how feared you are on your own, eh?"

Scarlett didn't have time to think about how he knew her. Only that the attacker Gruber had gone after seemed to be wearing some kind of protective gear. As though the cartel had known they'd need it.

Because they'd been expecting her.

She brought the gun up, aiming over her shoulder, and pulled the trigger. The bullet went wide by a mile. But the resulting percussion did what she'd hoped.

Her attacker jerked her to the left, his grip around her neck faltering. High-pitched ringing drowned out the sounds of Gruber's growls not thirty feet away as Scarlett swung the gun up.

Too slow.

Pain spiked through her hand as the weapon ripped free and hit the floor. Giving her the first look at the man standing in front of her.

Muñoz. Not just a construct of King's investigation. But in the flesh. Her heart threatened to beat straight out of her chest as she tried to gauge movement elsewhere in the warehouse. No more shouted orders. No more gunfire. As though the fight had already been lost before it started. "Where is Agent Elsher?"

"Right where I want him," Muñoz said. "As are you."

No. She launched forward with a kick of her own and elbowed the son of a bitch in the chest. With no impact. She swung her fist toward his face as hard as she could, but he shoved her backward.

She hit the ground. Air seeped from her lungs, but she wouldn't give up. She wouldn't stop. Not until she couldn't fight anymore. Scarlett pressed herself up and went in for another strike.

Muñoz caught her fist in his palm and squeezed, but she wasn't going to let him slow her down. She spun to dislodge his hold and rocketed her knuckles into his face.

Disoriented, Muñoz stumbled back, and Scarlett took advantage.

She wedged her toes into the crease between his abdomen and thigh and hauled herself higher up his body. Wrapping her calf around the back of his neck, she increased the pressure until he was the one who couldn't breathe. But it wasn't enough.

Muñoz dug his fingers into her legs and threw her off.

Gravity gripped her insides a split second before she hit a packing crate. Boxes of fentanyl and baby dolls did nothing to counter the pain overtaking her entire body, but she couldn't let herself give in. Clawing from the mess, she grabbed for the blade tucked in her cargo pants. She rolled until she hit the strength of Muñoz's ankles and hiked herself to her knees.

Stabbing him in the back of the thigh.

His scream filtered through his teeth, just before the lieutenant locked his hands around Scarlett's throat and dragged her to her feet. He was strong. Stronger than her, but she had something he didn't. The will to save lives. And there was nothing that would stop her from keeping her word to King.

"You're going to regret that." Muñoz backed her into the edge of the oversize metal support. "I'm going to take everything you love and kill it, Scarlett Beam. Those people you work with—even Agent Elsher and his son— I'm going to make you watch as I burn your entire world to the ground. Then I'm going to kill you."

She worked to pry his hands from around her neck, but his grip only seemed to intensify. White pinpricks invaded her peripheral vision. It was no use. He would strangle her if she kept trying to physically overpower him. Scarlett went for the blade lodged in the back of his thigh, but Muñoz had expected that, too. He swiped her attack away as easily as he swiped at a fly.

Then slammed his fist into her face. Once. Twice. The world went black.

HELL. HE'D MADE a mess of things.

Pain pulsed in the back of his neck as he dragged his chin from his chest. Like he'd fallen asleep sitting up. Guess he technically had. Though the falling asleep part hadn't been his choice.

King put too much momentum into his neck, and his head fell back to stare up into a too-bright glow of fluorescent lighting. The office wasn't much more than a storage closet with foggy glass in the door. It was bland and empty, apart from an old metal desk the likes of which he hadn't seen in over a decade.

Damn it. His head hurt, but his pride had taken the biggest hit. He'd been so convinced Julien was here—desperate to be there for his son—he'd rushed in without a second thought as to what might wait on the other side. The attack had come fast, and the next thing he'd known was unconsciousness.

And now Scarlett and her Dobermans were out there trying to fix this. For him.

He'd never been the kind of man who would ask the people around him to do something he wasn't willing to do himself. But this… This wasn't going at all as he'd hoped.

A smattering of items on the metal desk a few feet away caught his attention. Phone, wallet, keys, badge, business cards. All his. No sign of his sidearm, though. His attackers had stripped him of anything he could use to his advantage.

King tried to break through the rope scratching

through the layers of skin around his wrists. Muscles he hadn't used for far too long weren't interested in showing up for him now. He'd relied too heavily on his gear these past few years. All of which had been taken from him now. And it would cost him everything.

Shadowed movement shifted on the other side of the fogged glass. No sounds of gunfire or fighting. Nothing to suggest Scarlett and her dogs were still alive.

He needed to get out of here. Get them out of here. He'd brought her into this mess. He'd be the one to make sure she didn't pay the price. "Think, Elsher."

He studied every inch of the office. It looked as though it'd been stripped for parts. All this time he'd believed that original DEA operation had hurt Sangre por Sangre's growth. At least shut down one of their primary warehouses. Turned out, he, Adam and Eva hadn't done a damn thing to bring these bastards to a stop. The cartel had simply taken on a new face.

His head pounded in rhythm to his heart rate. Too hard. Too loud. Twisting his wrists opposite directions, he worked the rope digging in deeper, but there wasn't any bit of give. He was screwed in the leg department, too. No room for escape. The chair he was tied to wasn't anything special. Though steel posed a problem. Guess the Sangre por Sangre cartel had too many mishaps with wood. Or maybe they'd suddenly turned environmentally conscious. Decided to give back for once.

"And I'm the freaking tooth fairy," he said.

Oh, hell. He *was* the tooth fairy now. Julien had a loose tooth ready to come out any day now, and King would have to be the one to sneak into his room and leave a dollar beneath his kid's pillow without waking him.

No. He couldn't think about that right now. The thought of never getting to be the tooth fairy for his son only messed with his head.

There. On the back wall. A wire storage shelf stacked with paper boxes. No labels telling him what each of them housed, but it couldn't be paper.

He tipped his weight back onto two chair legs, his toes barely connecting with the floor. His shoulders screamed for relief, but King had to try. This was going to hurt, but it would be nothing compared to losing his son. Or Scarlett.

King shoved back against his toes. Gravity launched his stomach into his throat a split second before he hit the floor. The combination of the metal rim of the chair and his body weight threatened to break both of his arms, and he swallowed the scream ready to explode from his chest. He rolled onto his side, taking the too-heavy chair with him as he tried to catch his breath. That was going to leave a bruise.

Digging his heels into the floor, he shoved himself across the floor toward the shelf. Inch by agonizing inch. He was out of breath by the time he reached the base. Sweat beaded under his bottom lip. "Move, damn it." Though how he was going to get these boxes open without the use of his hands or feet was a mystery.

The shelf itself had been constructed of smooth stainless steel. No way to use the frame to cut through the rope. But the sharp edges where the grating held the boxes themselves might help. King leveraged one shoulder into the floor and circled his feet to the left, setting his back to the wire rack. And set his wrists against the raw edges of steel.

He couldn't move more than a few centimeters at a time, but that was all he needed. The fibers of the rope caught, and King put everything he had left into keeping the pressure on. Back and forth. Back and forth. He wasn't sure any of it did a damn bit of good, but he wasn't going to give in. Not to the cartel. And not to the doubt telling him he wasn't ever going to find his son. That he was too late.

A warning growl pierced through the fogged glass on the other side of the room. Shit. He was out of time. King scanned the room for something—anything—that would get him out of this chair, but it was no use.

The door kicked back on its hinges and slammed into the wall behind it. A cartel soldier fought with a Doberman at the end of a choke chain, trying to drag the animal into the room, but the K9 wasn't cooperating in the least.

Gruber—when had King figured out which was which?—wrenched his head from side to side as he dug his heels into the floor.

"Gruber," he said.

The dog set coal-black eyes on him. Accusatory. Scared. Pissed off to hell and back. The soldier managed to pull the Doberman fully into the room with a heavy tug. But if Gruber was here… Where was Hans? Where was Scarlett?

Another soldier fireman-carried the second dog into the room and not-so-gently deposited her onto the floor. Injured? Dead? King didn't know, but he sure as hell wanted to witness what Scarlett had done in return.

A scraping sound overrode Gruber's overly loud fight for freedom. A rhythmic sound that raised the hairs on the back of King's neck. A large man struggled to fit through the narrow door as he dragged something heavy and unconscious behind him. Recognition hit, and King's entire world tore apart at the seams.

Muñoz.

Age had gotten to Muñoz over the past ten years. Striations of gray chased back the muddied brown in the man's facial hair and eyebrows. The skin beneath those empty eyes sagged and folded as gravity didn't have much care for appearances, but there was still a hint of the man Muñoz had been. Physically lean, well-kept in the suit department. Much stronger than he wanted people to know. "Hello, Agent Elsher. I brought you a present."

Muñoz dragged the body forward, that thick accent carving into King's memory.

Scarlett hit the floor without protest. Unmoving. Blood dried beneath her nose and around her mouth. Gruber's low whine punctuated the ache in King's gut as he visually searched for a pulse or a chest fall. Something to tell him he hadn't gotten Socorro's security operator killed for nothing.

"Get him up," Muñoz said.

The cartel member who'd dropped Hans to the floor left the Doberman where she lay and closed the distance between him and King. Rough hands jerked King back to sitting, and feeling shot back into King's arms.

Despite the image he wanted to convey, that of a DEA agent who didn't give into threats, King couldn't control the tremors in his chin. He tried to breathe through it, to give his nervous system something other than Scarlett and Julien to focus on, but it was no use. Muñoz wasn't known for keeping hostages. Both Adam and Eva had learned that the hard way.

Palpable silence filled the room, only interrupted by Muñoz's advance. "How long has it been, Elsher? Ten years? You don't look like you've aged a day. You must take care of yourself." The lieutenant rounded behind him, lowering his face beside King's. "Such a waste."

King didn't answer. His gaze locked on Scarlett. She was alive. She had to be.

"You know, I've never understood all these elaborate tortures the people I work with like to use. The accelerants in tires. Countless days of beatings. Acid on the skin." Muñoz penetrated King's peripheral vision. The cartel lieutenant unsheathed a tactical blade, dark steel serrated in high peaks and valleys. The lights didn't even reflect off the surface. Not like King expected. "It's the simplest things that can get the point across."

Muñoz swiped the blade across King's thigh.

Stinging pain erupted faster than he expected and stole the air in his lungs. He bit back the scream trying to force its way free, but it was no use. His composure had been corrupted the second he set eyes on Scarlett. Blood rushed through the wound though the laceration was shallow compared to what it could've been. He stared straight ahead. Not willing to give Muñoz the satisfaction of breaking him.

A slap to one side of the face ensured King couldn't disappear. That he had to stay present. "There will be little for the DEA or your son to identify you as human when I'm finished, Agent Elsher. The only question is, will you give me what I want in time?"

King forced himself to take a breath.

"I want everything your partner and that bitch from ATF collected on me and my operation." The weight of Muñoz's attention intensified the pain in King's wound. One second. Two. The lieutenant nodded, backing off slightly.

The second cut went deeper. King couldn't contain the scream of pain this time. His agony filled the room and took Gruber by surprise. The K9 howled in unison, but the man handling the choke chain cut him off short.

King's heart rate skyrocketed. Sweat slipped down the sides of his face.

"Perhaps your partner's wife will tell me where Agent Dunkeld hid the information he gathered. Jen, right? And the girls. Beautiful, beautiful girls. I can see them doing very well for Sangre por Sangre." Muñoz turned to the cartel soldier hovering over Hans and hiked a thumb toward the door. The subordinate left the room without a word, closing the door behind him. "In the meantime, why don't I remind you of what I'm capable of?"

Shuffling sounded through the door, and then the cartel soldier carried Julien—kicking and punching—in his arms.

Just before Muñoz stabbed the blade down into the top of King's thigh.

Chapter Eight

The scream ripped her out of unconsciousness.

Scarlett's heart thudded too hard in her chest as fractions of memory invaded. She sank in to the prickling numbness in her shoulder as she tried to gauge the situation without giving anything away. Until she caught sight of Hans.

The Doberman wasn't moving. Didn't seem to be breathing.

Instant grief burned in Scarlett's eyes. Hot and heavy and encompassing. She was slightly comforted by the fact Gruber seemed to be giving the man at the other end of a choke chain everything he had. With any luck, her defender would get the upper hand. Two cartel soldiers had positioned themselves off to one side from what she could see through the crack in her eyelids.

Her breath lodged in her nasal cavity, forcing her to part her lips. Pain kept rhythm with the ache in her face. Muñoz. He'd broken her nose. The crust of blood stuck to her face, but she couldn't worry about that now.

A groan called to something deep and protective as she pinpointed the source of the original scream. King had been restrained. Wrists, hands. And now a blade stabbed into his lower part of his thigh. But he wasn't the only one suffering—a third soldier tried to keep hold of a little boy struggling in his arms.

Julien?

The breath rushed out of her as a thousand different escape scenarios took shape in her mind. Each of them more unlikely than the one before, but one thing was clear. No matter what happened in the next few minutes, she'd get them out. All of them. Scarlett kept her senses trained on each threat as she worked her free hand toward the inside hem of her cargo pants. Muñoz had most likely stripped her of every weapon they could find, but there was hope they hadn't searched past the surface.

"All I need from you, Agent Elsher, is the location of Adam Dunkeld's and Eva Roday's investigation files." The cartel lieutenant dragged a chair from behind an old metal desk that resembled more of a cartoon anvil than a place to get any work done, the vibration of which rumbled through her.

A forced exhale reached her ears as she waited for King's answer. The files? All of this—the deaths of two federal agents, the kidnapping of a ten-year-old boy—for information for an off-the-books investigation. What the hell had Agents Dunkeld and Roday uncovered?

King's groan turned into more of a growl.

"The files, Agent Elsher," Muñoz said. "Please."

"I've got a little itch. On the right side of this blade." A hardness Scarlett had never witnessed seemed to roll through King as he faced off with Muñoz. "Do you mind?"

A frustrated laugh punctuated Muñoz shoving to his feet. He threw his chair backward, barely missing one of the cartel soldiers stationed behind him. The lieutenant latched on to the blade and twisted it deeper into her partner's thigh.

The sound of King's pain etched deep into Scarlett's memory, to the point she would hear it every time she closed her eyes. It took everything she had not to get to her feet and find another home for that blade, but she'd already failed King once tonight. She wouldn't let it happen again. Gruber echoed King's lament and doubled the amount of agony washing through her.

She took the opportunity of distraction to make more progress on the inside of her waistband. To the razor blade she'd sewn into the fabric there.

It wasn't much, but it would have to be enough.

"No, to the right, Muñoz. I said to the right." A half laugh, half sob contorted King's usually even voice, shaking through him. His body wasn't going to be able to take much more. Shock hit everyone differently, but judging by the sweat coating his entire face and neck, Scarlett bet he didn't have much time before the laughs died. "Now everyone's going to know you died scratching my itch."

"I died?" Muñoz's voice didn't reflect his amusement.

"Yes." The tremors had settled in the past few seconds, giving her a raw look at the man holding out as long as possible to save the people he cared about. "Because no matter what you do, I'm not going to give you the location of those files, which means your bosses are going to hunt you down and cut you into tiny little pieces. And if you kill me, hurt my son or my partner, there will be nowhere for you to hide."

Scarlett pulled at the removable stitches and opened

up the small slit in the fabric of her waistband. The razor blade was inside. No bigger than half of her index finger but deadly enough in a pinch.

"That's where we disagree, Agent Elsher." Muñoz leaned down toward King's face, his back to Scarlett. "Because even after I get rid of your bodies, the DEA would still welcome me with open arms. They need what I know."

"Seems you've thought this through." King was struggling to breathe. Exaggerated. Short.

"I have." Muñoz, out of breath, sank down onto one knee, effectively ruining that pretty suit. Though maybe the blood stains on the right sleeve had beaten the floor to it. "Now, give me the location of the files, and I will at least let your son live."

But not Scarlett. Not Hans or Gruber. And not King.

Short bursts of breath escaped King's control as the dip in his brows suggested his inner fight with what might happen next. That intense gaze settled on her, and in that moment, she locked her full attention on him. And he knew. He knew that she wasn't going to give up or give in. Scarlett pulled the razor blade free, letting the sharp ends bite into her palms. She nodded. Just a little longer. That was all she asked.

Muñoz slapped the DEA agent's face, bringing him back to the present moment. "Do it soon enough, and Julien might even walk away in one piece."

King's laugh hiked his smile higher. Despite the blood loss and the overall agony he must have felt, he was going to hang on. To give them a chance of escape.

"You really aren't going to tell me, are you?" The cartel lieutenant wiped at his own brow, as though torture took more out of him than his victims.

"No." King shook his head.

"In that case." Muñoz shoved to his feet and kicked at King's chair. The agent tipped backward and landed with a hard thud against the cement floor. The lieutenant unsheathed a smaller blade than the one sticking out of King's thigh. "I'll start sending you back to the DEA one piece at a time."

Scarlett put everything she had into rolling, throwing herself into the back of Muñoz's legs, razor blade in hand. Her Kevlar vest threatened to slow her down, but that bright spot of determination was all she had to hold on to. Muñoz fell backward, slamming into the floor with his legs draped over Scarlett's side.

She swiped the blade across the tendon in the back of one ankle. "Can't have you following us."

Muñoz's scream outdid King's and called the other three soldiers to action. Only two of them were preoccupied with their captives. Julien and Gruber.

Eyes on the third soldier coming at her from across the room, Scarlett sawed through the ropes around King's wrists, then launched herself at the attacker closing in. "Get Julien out of here!"

The soldier pulled a gleaming steel blade and arced the knife down. Scarlett ducked, feeling every strike from her previous fight bruised into her sides and face.

Her attacker overextended, putting his back to her, and she took full advantage. She kicked him down as Gruber's growls grew louder with each passing second. She angled her back to the Doberman and the man at the end of Gruber's leash. Dragging her belt from her waistband, she wrapped it around her left forearm as the knifeman got back on his feet.

He came at her a second time, straight to the chest. Scarlett stepped to the side, letting him slide right past her. Into the cartel member at her back. The knife hit home, and the choke chain hit the floor.

Gruber was free, and he didn't waste a single second letting everyone in the room know about it. The Doberman launched at the knifeman as Scarlett caught the bastard's wrist and turned his own blade on himself. Shoving back with everything she had, she cornered both soldiers. Then kicked at the knee of the soldier with the knife.

Muñoz's screamed orders were nothing compared to the crunch of bone as the knifeman collapsed. Scarlett helped herself to his blade as the man who had held Gruber rushed forward with a knife of his own. She swiped at the bright steel in his hand but won a fist to the face instead. He launched at her, blade first, but missed her rib cage and embedded the knife into a metal filing cabinet as old as the oversize desk.

Scarlett knocked him out cold with an elbow to the face, but they were running out of time. The longer they stayed in this room, the sooner they'd be surrounded. The first soldier came at her again. She landed another kick to his chest and sent him backward, but it wasn't enough. He ran at her, and all she could think to do was tackle him to the floor. They hit as one, each struggling to get ahold of the knife in her hand.

Gruber latched on to the soldier beneath her and jerked his head back and forth to tear through clothing and flesh and anything else that might get in his way.

The resulting screams triggered a high pitch in her ears as she let the Doberman keep himself occupied. Adrenaline gave her the false sense of being able to tear through anything else that got in her way. She turned to deal with the last soldier holding Julien against his will.

To see King standing over the body with his son tucked behind him. The tactical knife from his thigh was in his hand. His shoulders hitched as he tried to catch his breath. Blood and sweat combined across his skin, deepening the carved lines in his face.

Scarlett took an initial step forward, all too aware that his will to protect and defend could turn on her any second. His wound was bleeding freely. There was no way they were going to make it without an intervention. Soft whimpers escaped from the boy hiding as much of himself as possible, and she tucked the knife in her hand into her back pocket. They weren't finished. There was an entire warehouse of cartel members standing between them and their escape. "You good?"

"Yeah. I'm good." King headed for the items piled on the desk and shoved them back into his pockets. The last—his badge—seemed to weigh on him heavier than all of them together from around his neck. Shuffling back toward Julien, he hiked his son into his arms. "Let's get the hell out of here," he said.

Just before he collapsed.

HE COULDN'T FEEL his leg.

King tried to get a hold on his vision as a blurred shape rushed toward him. Everything seemed to slow down and speed up at the same time. Muñoz clawed across the floor like the snake he was, blood trailing behind him in long streaks.

But it was the woman running for him with a dog draped over her shoulder that held King's attention. Her features remained out of focus until she was fisting one hand in his shirt and hauling him to his feet. There was no mistaking her for his partner. Or what she'd done to try to get them out of here alive.

"Scarlett." Her name was strangled in his mouth.

Gruber lunged for Muñoz and took the son of a bitch straight back to the floor. King struggled to shift his weight onto his good leg as Scarlett reached for his son's hand. The boy kicked and punched with everything he had, but the security operator took every hit with hesitation. She yelled something at King, running for the door.

And all he could do was follow. Because she was carrying them. All of them. Hans, Julien, him. With her strength. With her determination, and he couldn't help but want to stay close. She was aggressive and rational and passionate. She was everything he needed as King forced himself to take that first step, and she was the one who was going to get them out of here alive.

King maneuvered around Muñoz, who was still trying to claw toward the door. Bloody hands locked around his ankle and threatened to pull him down, but Scarlett had already gotten his son out the door with Gruber on her heels. King would do whatever it took to make sure they left together. Leg be damned.

Muñoz's mouth formed words drowned out by the hard pounding of King's heart. The bastard's fingernails dug through the fabric of King's pants and bit into skin. "Not…over."

"Yeah, it is." King shucked the lieutenant's hold and lunged out the door, both hands on the frame for support. His leg was dead. No telling how bad the damage was, but it didn't look good. Didn't feel good, either, but it was nothing compared with the alternative. His son would not witness King's murder by the same drug cartel that had sentenced his mother to death. Julien had suffered enough. King would take a stab wound any day.

Full-blown chaos exploded from every corner of the warehouse as their escape party left the safety of the office. Scarlett forged on up ahead, leading them to cover behind a row of boxes that wouldn't hold up against a hail of bullets for long. Julien jerked out of her hold, and she couldn't get him back, surveying the fight in front of them.

His son bolted out into the open. Terrified. Confused. With no place left to go.

King had no choice other than to set weight on his bad leg to catch the ten-year-old around the middle as he ran past. A scream ripped up the kid's throat and tore King's last remaining strength from him. No one should ever have to hear a scream like that. Dragging Julien into the nearest aisle, he set his son's back against his chest as bullets impacted the wall in front of them. King covered Julien's forehead with his hand, setting the kid's head against his chest. "It's okay. I've got you, Julien. I've got you. Do what I'm doing. Just breathe, buddy. Follow what I'm doing."

It was the same thing he told Julien every time the nightmares came for his son. The same comforting hold that kept the ten-year-old from hurting himself or others. And it was all King could do now.

Scarlett chanced a glance toward them, exposing the situation in her expression. They were out of options.

The realization hit harder than getting the news about Eva or the call about Adam. Because this wasn't a bunch of operatives that'd been thrown together in the name of public safety. The men and women he served with had signed on to risk their lives for the greater good, and as much as King would give his own life to save any one of them, this was his son at risk now. The only person he had left to care about in his world.

"That's right. Breathe like me, and soon it will all be over." He kissed Julien on the crown of his head. "We're going to get out of here. We're going to go home. I just need you to be brave for a little longer. Okay?"

Julien's grip left half-moon impressions in King's hand, as though the boy had marked him as his own. His son nodded.

Blood seeped from his wound and settled beneath his leg in a pool that got stickier and thicker by the second. The knife hadn't penetrated all the way through, but it'd done a hell of a job on the way in. King was bleeding out. Slowly. Minute by minute. And the harder he pushed himself, the sooner he'd have to let Julien go.

Scarlett's gaze dipped to his leg, then back to his face. Understanding seemed to hit as they sat there warding off bullets.

"You're doing great, buddy." King tried repositioning the bad leg, but the damn thing wouldn't move. Not an inch. The pressure in his chest reached an all-time high. No matter how hard King had fought to be the father Julien deserved, he wasn't going to make it out of this. Wasn't going to be there for his son. Not like he'd come to hope. "Now, you see that pretty lady with the dogs? Her name is Scarlett. She's the one giving the orders. I need you to do everything she says. She's going to make sure you're safe."

Scarlett let Hans slide down to the floor—gently. She kept low as she came to sit by King and Julien, her mouth trying for a smile as the world around them threatened to collapse. "Do you like dogs, Julien?"

His son nodded, though from the angle of his head, King bet the kid wasn't looking at her. And he wouldn't. Not until he started trusting her. It was only in the past couple weeks, King had gotten the pleasure of his son's eye contact. It'd meant so much then. More so now.

"This is Gruber. Funny name, huh?" Scarlett tucked the Doberman into her side and planted a kiss behind the dog's ear. "Would you like to pet him? He likes scratches behind his ears."

Julien reached forward, and King couldn't help but memorize this moment. Where the three of them had somehow created a solid bubble between them and the evil that waited on the other side of these shelves. His son massaged behind Gruber's ears, and the K9 flicked a long pink tongue against Julien's wrist.

"Aren't you lucky? That means he likes you." Scarlett locked her gaze on King. Neither of them wanted to say it, but leaving the truth unsaid didn't make it untrue. King wasn't leaving this warehouse. Not as long as he couldn't control this bleeding. Which meant he had to trust her to keep her word. She had to get Julien out alone. Scarlett turned her attention back to his son. "And because he likes you, he's going to do whatever it takes to keep you safe. So am I. Okay? No matter what. I promise." She extended her hand. Waiting.

And Julien took it. Which was a miracle in and of itself. King couldn't remember a single time his son had reached out like that. Not since he'd come to live with King. It was just one more piece of evidence of Scarlett's effect on people.

She brought the boy to his feet as she stood.

But Julien hung on to King's other hand, unwilling to let go.

Tears burned in King's eyes. This wasn't like dropping Julien off at school every day, worried something would happen that King couldn't fix. This was goodbye. And damn it, he wasn't ready. "It's all right, buddy. You've got your very own personal guard dog. Cool, huh? And Scarlett here is going to make sure no one can hurt you again. You go with them. I'll be right behind you."

He'd never lied to his son before, and it didn't sit well now, but King couldn't destroy this boy's world all over again. King kissed Julien's hand, giving it a small shake. "It's going to be scary, but you've got this. You're amazing and brave and as stubborn as they come." King was losing it. Going right over the edge of being able to let go. "Go on now. Before you know it, we'll be back at home in our own beds with a big bowl of popcorn and your favorite movie."

Shouts grew louder. Closer.

They were out of time together.

Julien fell into King's arms, squeezing harder than ever before, and King's heart hitched in his chest. Just before his son pulled away. One hand on Gruber's collar, the boy kept close to Scarlett as she backed herself toward the end of the aisle. That brilliant gaze cut through him.

"I'll protect him. I promise," she said.

"I know you will." In the short time they'd partnered together, he'd learned that was the kind of woman she was. A woman of her word.

King watched as they got to the end of the aisle. Scarlett bent down, gathering Hans into her side, and whispered something to Julien, who nodded before taking her hand.

"I'll hold them off as long as I can," King said.

His son turned back to look at him one last time. Just as he'd imagined his mom had done when she'd slipped free of his bedroom all those years ago. Hell, King couldn't help but see her in that boy's face.

"I love you, Julien. Don't ever forget that." King didn't care if the cartel heard him. All he had to do was give Scarlett and Julien and Gruber a chance to escape.

Julien didn't answer. But King saw it there. The softening, the glisten of tears. His son loved him, too. In his own way and in his own time.

Two months wasn't enough for King. Wouldn't ever be enough, but he sure as hell appreciated the time they had together in the last few minutes of his life.

Scarlett led Julien out of sight, Gruber taking his job seriously at his son's side. And they were gone. Leaving King to fight off Sangre por Sangre alone.

The door to the office swung open, one of Muñoz's men dead center in the frame. Gun raised and aimed.

But King wasn't going out on their terms. Just as he would bet Eva and Adam hadn't. The last reserves of adrenaline dumped into his veins.

King was on his feet.

He lunged.

And tackled the cartel soldier a split second before the gun went off.

Chapter Nine

The shot punctured through the rhythmic pounding of her feet and Gruber's nails against the asphalt. Every cell in Scarlett's body knew the source, and instinctively she slowed their escape. Hans's weight nearly pulled her to the ground.

A hundred feet. That was all that stood between them and the SUV, but the need to go back—to pull King out—gutted her. But she couldn't turn back. She'd given him her word she would get Julien out, and there was no way she'd put his little life at risk. Not now. "Almost there."

Midnight air sucked the sweat off her skin and from beneath her gear. She picked up the pace. Julien was breathing hard to keep up, but he was alive, and that was all that mattered. Scarlett remote-started the car. "Get in."

No other gunshots came from inside the warehouse. Nothing to suggest the cartel was still fighting off the threat that had penetrated their walls. Which meant…

No. She didn't want to think about that.

She helped Julien into the back seat and fastened his seat belt. She had to keep her word. Rounding to the cargo area, she laid Hans—still breathing—across the carpeted space as Gruber jumped inside to settle down next to his sister. Any second Muñoz would order his men to expand the search area. They'd be found. They had to leave. Now.

But Scarlett couldn't help but slow when she caught sight of Julien with his hand pressed against the window. Waiting for King to be right behind them as he'd promised. Why was it people always said that? *I'll be right behind you.* Knowing the circumstances would force them to lie?

She followed Julien's line of sight to the side door of the warehouse that nearly blended in with the metal sheeting. All but for a single overhead light outlining the exit. Two seconds. Three.

King wasn't coming through that door.

He wasn't going to be able to keep his promise.

Unless she helped him.

Scarlett collected the remaining ammunition and her backup pistol from the cargo area, her mind made up. Gruber would kill anyone who tried to get into this vehicle. She reached for the Doberman, sliding her thumb across his head. *"Pass auf."* Stand alert.

Setting her palm against Hans's rib cage, Scarlett took in the K9's heat to settle the nerves trying to win out over her determination. "Take care of them. Okay?" She grabbed for the steel Hux tool all Socorro operatives carried to get through push bar doors in case of emergency. Two wedged prongs would create a gap between the locking mechanism and the frame while the solid length of the tool gave her leverage to pry it open from the outside. Not entirely legal. But useful.

"Julien, I want you to stay in the SUV. No matter what happens, don't open this car door for anyone but me. Okay? I'm going to get your dad. I'll be right back."

She didn't wait for an answer. King didn't have that kind of time. She slammed the cargo area closed and locked the running vehicle. Couldn't have the state taking Julien from her because she'd left him in a hot locked car. The air conditioning would keep him cool enough. Scarlett tucked the tool beneath her arm as she loaded a fresh magazine into her weapon and faced off with the warehouse, every nerve in her body on fire.

She moved fast, closing the distance between her and the exit. Couldn't go back the same way they'd gone in before. Muñoz and the rest of the cartel were already on alert. She leveraged her shoulder against the metal sheeting of the warehouse, the absorbed heat of the day working bone-deep.

She glanced back at the SUV, imagining Julien watching her through the heavily tinted bulletproof glass. She could do this. She had to do this. For that boy. And for King.

Holstering her weapon, Scarlett angled away from the building and inserted the Hux tool between the door latch and the frame. A gap in the frame increased with every pull. Until the door snapped free altogether. She slid the tool along her forearm. Bracing herself for what came next. Aches pulsed in her face from the last time she'd squared off with the soldiers on the other side of this door, but it wasn't going to stop her now.

Scarlett breached into quiet. As though the entire warehouse were waiting for her to come in far enough so they could jump out and yell, *Surprise!* But there wasn't going to be cake at the end of this party.

She kept her back pressed against the nearest shelf, moving slower than she wanted to. Taking in every change around her. Where was King?

Movement caught in her peripheral vision from a gap between shelves in the aisle off to her right. Coming straight at her if she didn't move fast. Forcing her legs to pick up the pace, she jogged to meet the soldier leading with an assault rifle aimed level for anyone who got in his way.

Scarlett's knees protested as she crouched. One bullet would end this for all of them. She had to stay alive. Work smarter, not harder.

Wire shelves bit into the sensitive skin at the back of her neck as she waited. The soldier's boot crossed into the aisle.

Scarlett let the air out of her chest. And swung up with everything she had. The Hux knocked the rifle straight up, and a spray of bullets exploded into the ceiling. Like fireworks. Though this wasn't as pretty.

The soldier shoved her off.

She hit the floor and rolled, pulling her sidearm in the process. "Where is Agent Elsher?"

A low laugh and incredibly crooked teeth made dread pool at the base of her spine. Seemed this soldier liked to partake of the cartel's supply. He pulled an oversize blade from his back, swaying it back and forth in front of her. "You know the twenty-one-foot rule?"

Twenty-one feet. It wasn't as much as civilians might assume, but the rule was simple enough. Would she be able to get a shot off before he stabbed that blade through her? "I work for a security company. I'm pretty sure they taught that on the first day."

A gunshot exploded from behind the soldier, and his expression deadened right before her eyes. He collapsed to his knees. The blade pinged off the cement just before he fell face first. Revealing King standing behind him, weapon raised.

Sweat and blood and exhaustion clung to every inch of him as King's gun hand fell to his side. "You're not… supposed to be here."

Scarlett collected the discarded assault rifle from the floor, running to meet him. Another round of shouts told her there were more cartel members on the way. It was a big warehouse. No way to tell how many members were inside, but she didn't want to wait around to find out.

Slinging the weapon around her chest, she tucked herself underneath his left arm to keep King from eating the floor against his will. "I came to make sure you keep your promise to that kid."

"Where's Julien?" Two words made his priorities clear, and she had to admire that. He hadn't just taken on caring for a ten-year-old because a social worker and society expected him to step up as a father. He'd done it out of love. Raw, undying love for someone he barely knew.

"Safe. Come on. We need to get you out of here before you bleed out all over." She took the majority of his weight, in addition to her Kevlar and the rest of her gear. Her legs screamed for relief, but she'd trained and operated under worse circumstances. This was just a warm-up.

"Do me a favor." King shuffled forward at her lead.

"I'm kind of in the middle of the last favor you asked of me." She swung the rifle up as they passed each aisle on the way back to her entry point. "Not really sure I can take on much more at the moment. You know, facing off with a bunch of armed sociopaths and all."

King forced her to a halt. Pain and something along the lines of death infiltrated his expression. He swayed on his feet. Any second now, he wouldn't have the strength to stay upright. Hell, it was a miracle he'd gotten this far. "Tell Julien I'm sorry. I'm sorry I couldn't protect him the way he deserved."

Air lodged in her throat. Scarlett strengthened her grip on his T-shirt. "You're going to tell him yourself." She moved them forward. Fifty feet. Forty. They were almost there. She could see the outline of the door ahead. They were going to make it.

A gunshot exploded from behind them.

Searing pain thudded through her midback and shoved her forward. King lost his hold on her, and they hit the floor in a tangled heap of limbs. Agony spread beneath her waistband and up underneath her Kevlar vest. One hand stretched out in front of her, she reached for the door that would get them both out. Only it wasn't enough. Her lungs suctioned for air. The Kevlar had taken the hit, but she couldn't rush the recovery.

The gunman shouted something she couldn't decipher. Calling the rest of the shooters to his location.

No. She had to keep moving. Had to get King back to Julien.

"Scarlett." King's hand found hers.

"I'm fine." The lie slipped easily from her mouth, and right then she had her answer. People who promised they were right behind their loved ones in an impossible situation lied to make acceptance easier. To give hope. "We're going to make it."

Her heart thudded too fast at the back of her head, screaming for her to stop, to rest, to give up. But that wasn't her. Scarlett rolled onto her back and latched on to the rifle jutting into her rib cage. She squeezed the trigger, taking out the gunman advancing on them.

The soldier crumpled to the floor. A multitude of footsteps echoed off the metal warehouse walls. Three sources. Maybe more. This was her and King's last chance.

She latched on to King's hand as though it were a lifeline. It was. Pushing her upper body off the floor, she got her feet under her. Bruising intensity dug deeper into her back the more she aggravated the wound, but she couldn't stop. Not until she kept her promise. She reached for King, helping him stand. "We have to move. We have to go."

The door was right there. So close and so incredibly far away. The voices were getting louder. Closer. But she wasn't going to slow down. One foot in front of the other. And they were finally there. Pushing through the door she'd pried open, and then out into the night. They crossed the parking lot, leaning on each other for strength, but that strength was quickly running out.

Scarlett set her gaze on the SUV ahead. Only something wasn't right. The back door… It shouldn't have been open. Fear penetrated for the first time and intensified the pain in her low back. "Julien."

His son's name brought King's head up as they picked up the pace.

Desperation unlike anything Scarlett had felt before burned through her. She practically dove into the back seat of the SUV, hands spread wide in search.

But he wasn't there.

"Where is my son, Scarlett?" King nearly ripped the opposite door off its hinges. "You said...he was safe. Where is he?"

She clutched the SUV's frame as everything inside of her went numb. "He's gone."

THEY'D HAD HIM.

Julien had been right there in his arms.

Something heavy and uncomfortable seemed to be sitting on his leg. King couldn't move, and the instinct to fight bubbled up inside him. Pinpricks of numbness spread through his palms.

No. That didn't feel right, either.

A soft rhythmic beep broke through the pounding of blood in his head. Increasing. Like a heartbeat. This... wasn't him coming around tied to a chair after being knocked out cold. Something was different.

King fisted a handful of fabric as he forced his eyes open. Dim lighting and deep shadows played a game of dominance which neither was winning. There was the black outline of an open door off to his right. A blue glow came from a window next to it.

The room was small but private. The source of the rhythmic annoyance was right there beside his bed, along with whatever was monitoring the clear rubber tubes coming out of his forearm.

Hospital.

Made sense after taking a tactical blade to the thigh.

The memory of which created a deep ache he knew he couldn't actually feel. At least not with whatever pain meds they had him on. More like remembered pain.

And it was nothing compared to the anguish of finding Scarlett's SUV empty once they'd escaped the warehouse.

He didn't remember much after that.

His son was missing. Again. They'd been so close to bringing him home. King had promised him. Promised him he'd be safe. That everything would be okay as long as they were together. And now Julien knew his father was a liar.

King had to go back. Had to take a look at the scene in the daylight. Sangre por Sangre be damned. He wasn't giving up. Not on his son. Not on their future together.

King sat up higher in the bed, though his muscles had filled with lactic acid that made every move hell. Too long spent unmoving. Tremors shook through his arms as he put most of his weight into his upper body. The bed rails had been raised, and he grappled for the release. The remote control for the bed slipped off the edge of the mattress and slammed into the bed frame, but he didn't need it. He needed to get out of here, to find his son.

The bed rail dropped with an exaggerated crash in the silence of the room, but he got the damn thing down. He'd take that as a win. Cold worked up through his bare feet as he pressed them to the floor. He was out of breath. The machine tracking his vitals was going haywire. Damn it. How the hell was he supposed to walk out of here like this?

"If I'd known you were this bad at escaping, I never

would've let you follow me into that warehouse." Her voice urged him to lie back, relax into the bed and hang on her every word. As though it alone could get him through the pain. And the lies.

Scarlett.

A lethal dose of rage mixed with gratitude to the point he couldn't tell which way was up. She'd saved him. Kept Julien alive. Delivered on her promise. Yet if she hadn't come back for him, his son would still be safe. King twisted, putting her outline in his peripheral vision. He hadn't noticed her lying on the cushions shoved up against the window, but he knew enough about Scarlett now to know she only showed herself when she wanted to be seen.

Dryness graveled up his throat. "How…how long have you been sitting there watching me?"

"Long enough to know there's no way you're getting out of here without help." Her outline shifted forward, and he could see thin lines of light coming through the blackout curtains. Daylight. They'd made it through morning. "You can't go back, King. He's not there. I already tried."

"You tried." That rage wanted to keep burning beneath his skin, but it was nothing compared to the appreciation of knowing Scarlett had risked her life—twice—to bring Julien home.

The DEA wouldn't have done that. A failed mission meant escaping with the lives they had, regrouping and coming up with a new plan. Not trying to fix the one that nearly killed them in the first place. But he'd learned something else about her over these past two days. Scarlett Beam didn't accept defeat. Ever.

"We had him." Tears pricked in his eyes, and hell, he hated this feeling of helplessness, of powerlessness. Julien needed him at his best, and this…wasn't it.

Scarlett moved so gracefully, he barely heard her before the mattress dipped with her weight beside him. Damn it, she looked stronger than ever. As though the butterfly bandage across her nose had given her some kind of superpower while he was stuck in this broken body. "I'm sorry, King. I gave you my word I would get him out. I had him. He was safe. I could've brought him to Socorro, and there would've been no way for the cartel to get their hands on him. But I…"

"You couldn't leave me behind." How could King fault her for that? Choosing to save two lives instead of one? It was what any agent in her position would've done. Hell, he would have, too.

"I'm the reason he was taken again," she said.

King's senses adjusted enough for him to see her fist her hands in the fabric of her cargo pants. "You're the reason he's still alive, Scarlett." He set one hand over hers. Despite the low temperature of the room, a flurry of heat shot into his palm at the touch. The instinct to pull away charged through him, but there was something stable and balancing in that single touch at the same time. Something he needed. "Without you, we'd both be dead, and you know it."

Flashes of memory broke free of the pain med barrier, and his heart rate hitched higher. "I remember you carrying Hans out. Did she make it?"

"Hans is back at Socorro with the vet. She took a beating, but she's going to pull through. But Gruber…" Scarlett swiped a hand beneath her nose, then cringed in pain. As though she'd forgotten the break. "I left him to guard Julien when I went back into the warehouse for you."

"But he wasn't in the car, either." King remembered that now. The SUV had been empty apart from Hans's still frame. Which didn't make sense. "You think the cartel took him?"

"I searched that entire area after I brought you in." She shucked his hand from hers, leaning to one side to pull something from her pants pocket. "All Socorro K9s carry responders in their collars. They're even trained to trigger the emergency signal. Gruber activated his while we were in the warehouse, and Socorro responded."

She handed off a leather strap, and King worked his thumb over the worn leather pitted with adjustable holes. A metal rectangle was etched with some kind of lettering—Gruber's information if King had to guess.

"Only problem is, they were too late," Scarlett said. "All my team found was this about twenty yards from where we parked the SUV. I have to assume Sangre por Sangre knew our K9s have transponders embedded in their collars, and Gruber wouldn't let the cartel take Julien, so they took him, too."

"Why not just kill him and take my son without the fight?" King hadn't meant to say the words out loud. As much as he didn't understand the connection some people had with their dogs, it was obvious the Dobermans had fought like hell to protect Julien. And he wasn't going to forget it.

"I don't know. Maybe as leverage," she said. "But for what, I have no idea."

"I'm sorry, Scarlett." He handed the collar back, feeling heavier than when he'd woken up. "I know how much you care about those dogs."

"That's the job, isn't it? We risk our lives to protect the ones we care about, but nothing is permanent." Scarlett skimmed her fingers over Gruber's collar. "And this isn't over. I gave you my word I would bring Julien home, and I'm not giving up."

"Neither am I." King reached for the side table to give himself something to hold on to. Shoving to stand, he put all his weight onto his good leg as he slapped a hand over his cell phone. "I need to check in with my supervisory agent. Get a raid party together to breach the warehouse and confiscate those shipments of fentanyl."

"King, you can't." Scarlett rounded back into his vision, supporting him with a hand beneath his elbow. She was everything he needed right then, and everything he'd missed in a partner.

"Not sure if you know this, but that's actually my job." He scrolled through his contacts and hit his SSA's information. The screen went black and started a countdown as the line rang.

"No. I mean the DEA is already aware of our attempt to recover Julien. They know about the drugs, too," she said.

"How?" The answer was already there, waiting for his brain to break through the pain killer haze and catch up. Scarlett had said she'd gone back. Her team had recovered Gruber's collar. King searched for his clothing, but it was no use. The authorities would've already taken them as evidence. "Where are the pills I took from the shipment we opened?"

"The DEA took custody of them after I provided my

statement. One of their agents showed up dead yesterday morning, and another's son was abducted. They weren't just going to sit on the sidelines." Her expression collapsed. "They know everything, King. I didn't have a choice."

Defeat stole the last remaining energy he'd reserved as King sank back onto the bed. A voice cut into the surrounding silence. Voicemail. He ended the call. His SSA wasn't going to answer. "How bad is it?"

Her voice softened. Trying to ease the blow, he imagined, but he already sensed what was coming. "The DEA has put you on suspension, pending an investigation into what you've been putting together on the cartel the past couple of months. They confiscated everything in Agent Dunkeld's home office, including the case he and Agent Roday were working together. The FBI is on its way to handle Julien's kidnapping, and Socorro has been ordered to step aside."

A headache spread from the base of his neck, threatening to break him all over again as the last remnants of his life shattered in front of him. He wasn't just on the verge of losing Julien. His job was at stake, too. "All right. If the DEA knows about the warehouse, they can put together a raid party. Match the pills we took to the shipments in those boxes."

"They breached the warehouse about an hour ago, King, but it was cleaned out." Scarlett shook her head. "Everything that can corroborate our statements is gone."

Chapter Ten

It shouldn't have been possible. An entire operation gone within a few hours? With his injury, Muñoz couldn't even walk. How the hell could he have coordinated cleaning out that warehouse? And where did he run to?

The logistics didn't really matter. King's son did. They'd been so close to bringing him home, but now Julien seemed farther away than ever.

Scarlett flipped through another series of photos put together by Agents Dunkeld and Roday for the thousandth time. It hadn't taken much to create copies of the off-the-books investigation file and make it look like the original. The DEA could have the collection they left in Dunkeld's home. She'd piece this together with the raw notes she and King had uncovered in Dunkeld's office vent.

Only they were looking at the same information that'd brought them to that warehouse in the first place.

Sangre por Sangre was no longer accepting their position on the bottom rung of the ladder with their cocaine deals to high school students and underage recruiting parties. They were moving up in the world. Into fentanyl. And if history taught Scarlett and her team anything, it was the cartel didn't have the means or the resources to get the warehouse up and running on their own. Not like that. But who in their right mind would partner with a cartel?

Her head nodded forward without her permission, the photograph in front of her blurring for a moment. Any second now, her head would collide with the stir-fry she'd pulled from the fridge, uneaten. The pain in her face seemed to shift with gravity, and Scarlett leaned back in the chair. She couldn't stop now. Not while Julien and Gruber were still out there. She'd made a mistake, and she had to be the one to fix it. Before that little boy's body was the next to show up on her doorstep.

"When was the last time you slept?" King looked as beaten as she felt. He shuffled into the too-small galley kitchen of Socorro's headquarters, a crutch shoved under his arm. His facial hair had grown in over the past couple of days, revealing a single patch of lighter hair on one side. He'd changed out of the tight hospital gown that revealed more than she'd expected at the back and into what looked like a thrift store T-shirt with a popular cartoon cat and a pair of jeans that didn't quite fit around his waist. But damn it all to hell, being his center of attention still got her heart pumping.

She readjusted in her seat, leaning her elbows against the table to give her more stability. With a shake of her head, Scarlett put herself back in the game. It was the only thing she could do. They both knew who he blamed for losing Julien last night. "Shouldn't you still be in the hospital? How did you get here?"

His laugh shouldn't have had any effect on her while she was this tired, but Scarlett couldn't help but feel the tension seep out of her spine. "You'd think breaking out and calling a ride-share would be more difficult under the circumstances."

"You just signed the discharge papers against your doctor's orders, didn't you?" She didn't have the strength or the resolve to banter with him right now. Not with part of her brain focused on the file, another wishing she was asleep in her room down the hall and the last wondering when Ivy Bardot would descend from her throne on high to cut her from the team.

Scarlett had acted irresponsibly going to that warehouse without backup, without a strategy in place and without clearing it through Socorro first. And King's little boy had paid the price for her mistake. That in and of itself was unacceptable. She'd endangered lives. All to neutralize her own guilty past. Scarlett rubbed the sleep from her eyes. "You called a rideshare?"

"You wouldn't believe the going rate to get out here. Does Socorro expense travel for its operatives?" King dragged himself through the kitchen and pulled a chair from the end of the table that didn't get much communal use. He lowered himself down with the help of the crutch, his injured leg stretched out in front of him, and she couldn't help but imagine him here between assignments, as part of the team. A knife to his thigh had sliced through muscle and tendon, but the prognosis was better than they'd expected. He'd fully recover given enough time and physical therapy. "Scarlett, what are you doing?"

"I took photos of all of Agent Dunkeld's notes from his office. I'm going back through them. There are references here I haven't been able to make sense of yet.

Random letters. Almost like it's some sort of code, but one I haven't seen before."

The letters seemed to jump off the page every time she looked away, as if they were calling her. Or maybe she was just hallucinating. She scrolled through another set, these written in more feminine handwriting. Eva Roday's, if she had to guess.

"My gut says if we manage to find the key to decode them," she said, "I think we'll have a better idea of where we stand. Maybe even who is partnering with the cartel and where they might be located."

"You need to go to sleep."

His voice intensified that exact need, like her body had been waiting for his permission. But she couldn't stop. Not yet. Not until she had something to bring back his hope. Because she'd been the one to kill it. The second she'd gone back for King in that warehouse, she'd broken her promise to get Julien out safely. And she couldn't live with that for the rest of her life. She could barely live with herself as it was now. "I'm fine. I just need… I just need some coffee."

"Coffee can fix a lot of things, but it can't fix this." King's breathing picked up as he got back to his feet. He wedged the crutch beneath his arm with one hand and offered the other to her. "Come with me."

His voice had been so clear a few minutes ago but refused to register in her brain now. He was right. Coffee wouldn't fix this. Neither would changing out her contacts or taking a cold shower. She'd given everything she had to recovering Julien, and she'd failed. Throwing herself back into the investigation wasn't going to change that.

Her attention latched on to the pattern of lines in his palm. Just before she slid her hand into his.

King didn't do much in the way of helping her up—couldn't in his condition—but the intention was still there. After everything they'd been through together, he wanted to help her. As a unit, they shuffled back through the kitchen and into the corridor before King pulled up short. "I'll be honest. I have no idea where I'm going. Every hallway looks the same to me."

"I've got you covered." Scarlett led him to the right, then took a left and shoved through a door at the end of the hallway. A deep heaviness clung to her legs as she caught sight of her bed. King-size suddenly had all new meaning as she considered whether or not to invite him inside. But her boundaries had been broken the moment she went back in to save him from Muñoz and the rest of the cartel.

Only this time King made the choice for her.

Maneuvering inside the room, he surveyed the space with its floor-to-ceiling windows making up two walls, the bed jutting out from the wall to their right and the simple layout with the bathroom and closet tucked out of sight. "This is…a lot of pink."

He was right. The upholstered headboard had been custom-made. The faux fur rug had been on sale in one of those huge home decor stores that were popping up all over. Pinks, whites and navy colors created a palette that made her happy every time she walked into this room. It was hers. Every inch. Hers. "Don't you have a favorite color?"

"Black shows the least amount of blood. Does it count if it's just good logic?" King was still taking it all in.

The roses on the nightstand with a stack of books she'd read a thousand times. The built-in wardrobe where her gun safe was installed. He studied it all as though he was trying to understand the pieces of this room that made her...her.

And she liked it. Him being here. Trying to figure her out. Not in the way so many others had—how she could be of use, how she could benefit an operation—but pure curiosity.

"Sure." Suddenly blood seemed to drain from her upper body, pooling in her legs.

"Hey. I've got you." And then he was there, his hands anchoring around her waist. She wasn't sure how he'd moved so fast with that leg barely out of surgery, but it didn't really matter. "You've still got blood on you. I'll grab you a change of clothes."

Every cell in her body wanted to collapse as he led her to the edge of the bed and set her down.

Bending at the waist, he leveled his gaze with hers. "Don't move."

She wasn't sure she could even if she'd wanted to. Her body had hit a wall, and there was nothing that was going to get her to the other side until she gave in. Her pulse pinged a steady rhythm underneath the butterfly bandage across her nose as her partner pried the built-in doors wide.

King returned to face her with a set of her favorite pajamas in hand. Silk shorts and an oversize T-shirt. Ridiculous, really. That someone like her—someone who thrived in knowing and exploiting the enemy's weakness and who'd become comfortable with the violence that ensued—needed her pajamas to be soft. That she relied on that small bit of comfort every night.

He tossed the crutch on the bed, his weight on his good leg as he took a seat beside her. Hints of soap tickled the back of her throat. He'd showered—most likely at the hospital—and she couldn't help but wonder if she smelled anything close to clean. "Lie back and give me your foot."

She didn't have it in her to argue as the mattress came to meet her, and she dragged one foot away from the floor.

He grasped it between both hands, and a flurry of nervous energy spiked through her. There was a lot he could do with that one foot given the chance. But King wouldn't hurt her. That was how it worked when you went to war together. When you saw past the mask a person wore for the world, you got to witness the truth of them. And she knew King Elsher.

He tugged at the laces of her boot and slipped the heavy gear free, and Scarlett couldn't help but let her anxiety win. This was…slow. Uncomfortable. Out of her range of experience. No one had taken this kind of care with her since before her discharge from the army, and she wasn't sure what to do with it.

"Now the other one," he said.

She followed his orders as relief spread through her socked foot and nearly sighed as he dropped her other boot to the floor. He reached for the elastic of her socks and started pulling them free, one by one, but Scarlett bolted upright to stop him from going farther.

King waited. Held perfectly still until she made the decision. "I've got you. No matter what happens."

The words slid through her defenses as easily as the blade had gone through his leg, and she lay back down. Cool air added relief between her toes…just before King started massaging away the tension in her heel and the ball of her foot.

And she drifted to sleep.

KING COULD SPEND the rest of his life in this bed. He could even ignore the pink pillows underneath him, as long as he didn't have to give up this view.

Of Scarlett. Of her hair trailing around her shoulders and into her face. The clock on her nightstand warned him he was wasting time, but he couldn't seem to stop memorizing the way she'd lost that defensive edge while asleep.

She was beautiful. Definitely stronger than him, and more than he'd initially judged when they collided in the morgue—hell, when was that? Two days ago? The bruising fanning out from around her nose had darkened to shades of blue and purple but didn't take away from the spread of freckles peppered across her cheeks. He'd counted them. Over and over while she slept. One hundred and thirty-eight of them, each distinctive in its own right. Each one perfect.

"If you're going to keep staring at me like a serial killer stares at his prey, I'll require breakfast." Scarlett's voice cracked, but she gave him a half smile. Bright green eyes locked on him, and everything outside of these four walls didn't seem so important. "I like bacon."

"If that means I have to find my way through this maze back to the kitchen, you're out of luck." King's laugh rolled through him easier than it should have.

He'd been suspended from the DEA for running an off-the-books investigation into a cartel. The last woman he'd partnered with had been murdered in her own home. Adam had been tortured and slaughtered, and his son had been kidnapped. There shouldn't have been room for the lightness flooding through him. But Scarlett somehow made that possible.

She reached out, her fingertips brushing against the stubble across his chin. Heat cut through him, blistering and driven by something he hadn't experienced in a long time. Desire. "I believe in you."

The second laugh hurt more than it should have. His pain medication had worn off sometime during the night, but exhaustion had won out. Until now. He felt every blow as clearly as when they'd landed. In his ribs, his hands, his leg. They both knew getting lost in these halls wasn't going to end well for him.

Scarlett lowered her palm to his chest, directly above his heart. "I don't remember changing into my pajamas. Last night, did we…"

The question hung between them, and King didn't really have an answer. On the surface, it was easy. They hadn't slept together, but there was a part of him that was convinced they had. Mentally, emotionally. She'd trusted him to touch her, to take care of her, and while he didn't know her past as well as his own, King got the feeling that didn't happen often. If rarely. "No."

Her mouth formed an O for a split second. Surprised? Disappointed? Grateful? He couldn't tell. Scarlett pushed upright, angling long, lean legs over the edge of the bed. "Thank you. For getting me here."

"Figured you'd probably pass out at the dining table

with your tablet stuck to your head." While that may have been true, he also knew that keeping her from falling asleep in the communal dining room had little to do with it. "Wanted to save you the embarrassment."

She laid her head back on the pillow. Silk. Another element of this personal space he hadn't expected. Everything he'd known about Scarlett Beam up until this point had given him ideas of a dusty room with little to no personalization. A waystation between here and wherever she ended up next. But this…

This single room felt like a piece of home. Cared for. Lived in. Hell, he and Julien had been living together for nearly two months, and their place looked nothing like this. Didn't feel like it, either. As much as he wanted to credit the decor, King understood that all this warmth came from Scarlett. She was the one who added life to every room she walked into. Including the one where he'd been bound, interrogated and stabbed.

Scarlett tucked her hands beneath her chin, studying him. "Is this what you really look like in the morning?"

"Disappointed?" he asked.

"Not at all. I can finally see your face without all those tight lines in it." Her smile stretched from one side of her face to the other. The effect released her own set of tight lines from around her eyes and hitched his heart rate into overdrive. There was something about that smile. About that smile in this place, in this bed.

"I'm not sure if I'm supposed to take that as a compliment or an insult." He itched to close the small space between them, to feel her without a Kevlar vest getting in the way. To experience that heat she generated not just in his hand the few times they'd touched but over his entire body.

The truth was, he hadn't felt anything for a long time. And painkillers had nothing to do with it.

King reached out, sweeping long red hair behind her shoulder. His finger brushed against the underside of her chin, and Scarlett closed her eyes as if she'd been waiting for that physical contact as long as he had. Hell, she was so damn beautiful like this. Raw. Without any threats driving her from minute to minute. Right here, right now, she looked…at peace.

And despite the danger and the violence and the worry outside of this room, King felt the echo of that peace for the first time in… Damn, he couldn't remember how long. When his life hadn't become his job. When he hadn't been blindsided by a ten-year-old who'd been kept from him for the past ten years. When he hadn't lost the closest thing to a best friend he'd had. How long ago was that?

Seconds blurred together as they lay there. King wasn't sure how many. Didn't matter. Because he finally had the chance to breathe. To slow down. To just… be. In this bed he wasn't a DEA agent, the cartel didn't exist, he wasn't a father, and he wasn't grieving the loss of the loss of his job or everyone he cared about. He was King. A guy who'd dreamed of being a hero all his life, who'd fallen in love for the first time as a junior in college and had his heart broken, whose bucket list included things like visiting the Grand Canyon and seeing a real-life volcano and running a marathon. Someone who didn't feel the need to protect everyone and everything all the time, his own happiness be damned. Here, he was that man. Because of her.

King swiped his thumb beneath her chin, memorizing the feel of her skin, of a thin scar he hadn't noticed until now. He ran the pad of his finger over it a second time. She'd told him not to ask about the scar across her stomach, and he'd do as she asked. "What about this one? Will you tell me about that?"

"You're going to laugh at me." Sliding her hand over his, Scarlett pressed her face into his palm. "My nana used to make my cousins and me take naps when we were growing up. My mom and my aunt were working single moms at the time, and the four of us cousins would get dropped off at my nana's house. At the time I didn't understand why we had to take naps, but looking back I can see she just wanted a break. She was the one who needed the nap, and she didn't trust us to let her sleep without getting into trouble."

"You were one of the kids that got into trouble, weren't you?" He could see it now. Her curiosity, her determination to challenge and learn and figure the world out for herself. Nothing had changed in that sense.

"You're not wrong." Her laugh shook through his hand, real and bright. "We'd all pile in her king-size waterbed, but I never actually went to sleep. Instead, I would keep my brother and my cousins from going to sleep by poking them in their faces. Turned out, they didn't like that so much. My brother scratched me, leaving this scar, and I never poked him in the face again."

"Here I thought you were going to tell me you'd sneaked out of bed and gone to do something against the rules. Like climb the pantry for cookies. Seems more your style." He'd meant it as a joke, but the smile disappeared from her face.

Scarlett drew his hand along her neck, down over her collarbone. His fingers trailed between her breasts and over her stomach, lifting the hem of her shirt to expose the angry jagged pink line underneath. "The last time I broke the rules, my unit turned on me."

He didn't know what to say to that, what to think. "Your unit?"

Her gaze dipped to the raised scar tissue. "We were stationed in the Middle East. Security. Our job was to keep everyone safe, escort any high-value property on and off the base, investigate criminal activity, the works, but it turns out, the best people to break the rules are the ones who are there to enforce them."

Her skin warmed against his, her breathing coming faster, and King couldn't keep his distance any longer. Shifting, he closed the space between them and speared his fingers into her hair. "Hey. You don't have to do this. You don't have to trust me with this."

"But I do." She brought her gaze to his. Clear and soft and brilliant. The kind of eyes that could see right through him. And, damn it, King wanted her to see him. To be someone she could know and rely on in a world where she gave so much of herself to everyone else. "Which seems like a very dumb idea on my part, but here we are."

"Here we are," he said.

"I noticed things. Whispered conversations between a couple members of my team while we were on shift. I didn't think anything of it at first. Our unit wasn't exactly tight. More of a bunch of misfits thrown together, and I figured they had a closer relationship. They were friends, and I was the rookie. We got along. Drank together, told war stories and played Monopoly off duty, so I figured it was just a matter of time." Her next laugh wasn't as real as the last and died almost as quickly as it escaped. "But then I noticed a routine whenever the rangers brought in confiscated goods from their missions."

"What kind of goods?" He hadn't meant to ask, but it seemed important.

"Weapons, money." Scarlett tightened her hold on his hand. "Drugs. It didn't take me long to put it together. They had a protocol they followed whenever one of those shipments came in to be processed, and we were the ones in charge of processing."

"They were helping themselves." King pressed his thumb into end of her scar, where the tissue had built up more than the others. "What did you do?"

"Threatened to rat them out to our commanding officer and have them all court-martialed. Problem was, he was in on the operation, too." Her voice softened as she studied the line across her stomach. "And then one night, he decided he couldn't risk me telling anyone."

Chapter Eleven

She hadn't told a single soul.

Not outside of the court of JAG lawyers and the judge who'd been all too ready to throw her in the darkest hole after everything that went down.

Scarlett didn't want to think about any of that. About what had happened after she'd woken soaked in her own blood. She wanted to be in this bed. With King. He'd told her they hadn't slept together, but this somehow seemed far more intimate than mutual pleasure. As though she'd allowed him to dig through the scar across her stomach and peek inside. She'd never forget these moments. No matter what happened.

"How did you make it out of that alive?" he asked.

"I don't remember." It was the truth. She should've died from her wound. Part of her did and was continually trying to convince her none of this was real. That she'd been sent to purgatory to fight an impossible opponent for the rest of eternity. If she believed in things like that. Her brain provided the memories she'd tried to shove into a box at the back of her mind for over a year. "I remember my CO coming at me with the blade. I fought him off. As hard as I could. But it wasn't any use. I remember the knife going in. It burned more than I expected. I'm sure you can relate."

"A little." His thumb followed the length of her scar, back and forth, back and forth. Trying to hypnotize her. And it was working. Keeping her in the moment. Giving her an anchor when it would be so easy to let go and fall into the past.

She'd never had that before. Someone to hold on to. During her military career, she'd believed deep in her core that her unit would have her back. No matter where she was assigned. But that belief had been cut out of her. Literally. "He left me to bleed out. Stood over me until I lost consciousness to make sure, I guess. But next thing I knew, I was waking up in a small hospital room barely holding itself together. I was off base. I could tell that much right away. The surgeon who stitched me back together didn't even speak English. The army took my being off base as an act of treason. I was branded AWOL within hours."

"They charged you?" Distinct lines deepened between his eyebrows.

"After my unit was sent to find me, yeah." Her pleas echoed through her head as the scene played out like it had happened yesterday. "I tried to run, but the hospital I was brought to didn't have the resources to give me any pain medication. It hurt too much to move. I could barely stand on my own after what happened. So I was court-martialed. Dragged back to base. My CO stood in front of the judge, the attorneys and everyone in that room and told them he'd uncovered a smuggling operation within his own unit. That I was the ring leader, and he'd tried to stop me."

"And most likely used the fact you ended up in an off-base hospital to prove you were a flight risk," King said.

He was good at this. Putting the pieces together. It was what made him such an excellent agent, and she couldn't help but admire that. Maybe if she'd been as committed to looking at the people closest to her as she did for outside threats, none of this would have ever happened. Maybe she could've seen the end of the tunnel before the train hit her.

King's breathing had grown shallow, matching hers, and Scarlett wondered if his heart was threatening to pound straight out of his chest like hers. If his hands were sweating like hers. Probably not. This wasn't his story. It was hers. Dark and violent and full of secrets she'd hidden inside herself. But King made her feel safe. Good, even. Like someone worthy of being in his and his son's orbit. That feeling called to something deep and closed off inside of her. Something she'd left untouched for...forever.

"I was sent to the base hospital. Under guard. Handcuffed to the bed. No matter what I said, no one would listen. Not even my defense attorney. I didn't have any proof of my claims, and my CO knew it. And having me in custody gave my unit enough time to slowly shut things down in case someone else caught on. Lucky for me, I was isolated. No chance for them to slip by and finish the job."

"The investigators had to have found evidence somewhere. Someone must've come forward with information." King slid his hand along her hip, and instant defensiveness carved through her. But she was more convinced than ever he wasn't the threat. It was her own vision of herself. The crystal clear version of the woman who failed to bring Julien home as she'd promised. "You're here. You're with Socorro instead of in some prison the military keeps off the books."

"It was Granger." A chill tremored through her as she realized King had gotten closer. Mere inches between them.

He was absolutely beautiful. Impossible to look away from. Dangerous in his own way, but only to her sense of mission. Even so, she didn't want to pull away. She wanted to taste his mouth and didn't even care if that was weird. Had she ever wanted to taste someone before?

"We were stationed overseas at the same base," she said. "Overlapped by a few months as he worked counterterrorism in that part of the world for a brand-new private military contractor that hadn't gotten on its feet yet. I didn't know about him until I was being released from custody and handed my discharge."

"He's the one who brought you to the hospital. Gave the judge proof you weren't involved in the ring?" he asked.

She didn't really know how to answer that. Not with so many pieces still missing. "I know he found me in that hangar. If Granger hadn't been there, I would've died. He told me later he was already aware of the smuggling ring. He'd been closing in. And that made my CO desperate. Granger had gone in to that hangar to find the confiscated goods my unit stashed. Instead, he found me. Later, when he offered me a job working for Socorro, I took it without looking back. And here I am."

"Here you are." King's voice softened. His fingers brushed against her lower back and dug into the skin there. "Keeping your team and everyone else you care about safe."

"Almost everyone." She expected the past to rush into the present, to take these electrically charged moments from her, but it didn't. It stayed where it was supposed to. Firmly behind her. And left her all too aware of the hole consuming her from the inside. Which shouldn't have been possible as long as King held on to her.

"We're going to get them back, Scarlett. Both of them. Julien and Gruber. Together." Before she had a chance to argue, King crushed his mouth to hers. Claiming her. Fiercely. Intensely. As though he needed her as much as she needed him. And it didn't make sense. But his kiss was slick and hot and sweet, and all common sense had gone out the door the moment he touched her.

He angled his head, accessing her more deeply, and Scarlett had the impression if he hadn't been holding on to her waist, she would've fallen right off the bed. Heat charged up her neck and seeped into her face.

She'd kissed a few good men in her lifetime, starting at fifteen when her mouth had been full of braces and her boyfriend's bad breath. None of those compared to this. Her body responded as though she'd been waiting months—years—for this moment. Maybe all of her life for this kind of desire, and parts of her body she'd never fully engaged with were starting to wake up.

She met him stroke for stroke, with each ferocious pass of his tongue, and managed to keep the pain in her nose from taking over. Her heart thundered in rhythm with his, her whole body shaking for release as she clamped a hand onto the back of his neck and refused to let him separate from her. She was supposed to be in control, on alert for any kind of threat, but King made her feel desperate. Wanted. Whole.

Her body pressed against his from chest to toes. She was ready. For this. For them. For his forgiveness.

A knock punctured through the pounding in her temples, and King broke the kiss. "Expecting someone?"

"Not unless that's the breakfast I asked you to get." The pressure that'd tried to suffocate her since being forced to get King to the hospital last night had lightened. To the point she was able to take a full breath for the first time in hours.

"Can you have food delivered here?" he asked.

"Only if you want to traumatize poor delivery drivers." She released her hold, hating the emptiness in her gut that followed. But as much as she wanted to pretend these walls could protect them forever, reality didn't play that way. Hernando Muñoz was still out there. Still terrorizing the people of New Mexico, increasing his reach by merging with an unknown partner and holding a ten-year-old boy against his will.

Scarlett left the warmth of the man in her bed and padded to her bedroom door. Every muscle in her body ached with a reminder of her failure. She opened the door to Granger on the other side. "You have something for me?"

The counterterrorism agent handed off a single piece of paper. "You were right. We were able to trace the signature in the fentanyl pills you recovered from that warehouse back to a supplier."

"I thought you said you handed the evidence over to the DEA." King straightened to the edge of the bed but didn't bother trying to stand with his wound.

"I did. All but one of the pills." Scarlett read over the report of ingredients broken down line by line, looking for the one that would give them everything they needed: the cartel's new partner. "Once we breached that warehouse, there was no way Sangre por Sangre was going to stick around for the authorities to confiscate that much product. Given how much fentanyl is worth on the street, I'd say we uncovered a six-million-dollar operation. That kind of loss would destroy the cartel and any chance Muñoz had of making it out of there alive."

"So you kept one of the pills to have tested." A hint of admiration reached through the buzz he'd left behind from that kiss. "The DEA will be running their own tests. They're going to find out where those drugs came from."

"Yes, but federal crime labs take weeks to process evidence, and they're certainly not going to know where to look before we do." Bingo. The last ingredient. Scarlett glanced up at Granger to confirm the dread seeping through her. "Are you sure?"

"Had Dr. Piel run the results twice. She says it's not a mistake. We can do it again, but we're going to need another source. She went through the single pill you gave us. But unless you know of someone else using dextromethorphan in their fentanyl, I think we have our answer as to which organization Sangre por Sangre is using for new product."

"Dextromethorphan." King grabbed for his crutch and dragged himself to their position at the door. She handed off the toxicity results, and his gaze locked on the paper in his hand. "I only know of one organization that uses that as a signature in their product."

"Yeah. Me, too." Scarlett wanted to sink back into bed, to rewind the past few minutes and pretend wolves weren't waiting at the door all along. "Sangre por Sangre has teamed up with the largest triad in the world."

THE TRIADS CONTROLLED the drug trade through bribery, extortion and murder in the extreme. To the point western law enforcement couldn't even penetrate the organizations without inside help. They were the sole hands-off source of the opioid crisis ripping through the world.

And Sangre por Sangre had taken them on as a partner.

Providing them with unlimited resources in product, weapons and manpower. New Mexico would never stand a chance once the cartel took full advantage.

King couldn't just sit here. He dressed as quickly as his leg allowed. The wound was pulsing, trying to hold him back, but this new intel wouldn't wait for him to recover. The cartel was in over their heads, and his son was stuck in the middle. "Adam and Eva must've figured out the connection. They were getting too close to exposing the triad's involvement."

King aggravated the stitches in his leg, and he fell back against the mattress. Nausea surged as pain stabbed through his thigh, and all he could do was wait for it to pass. Sit here. Useless in his own body. "Damn it."

"Take it easy." Scarlett was there, securing her hands around the back of his calve. "That wound isn't going to magically fix itself in under twenty-four hours, King. You've got to give it some time."

"I don't have time." He hadn't meant his explanation

to sound so harsh, but King couldn't help it. They were running out of time. Julien was running out of time.

"I know." She massaged her fingertips around the wound, careful not to touch anywhere close to the bandages. "That's why I had Granger take what we know upstairs. Ivy and Socorro have been taking a lot of heat as to why the cartel only seems to be getting stronger despite our efforts to take down the key players. Now we know the answer. They're not the only ones we're up against, and I have a feeling it's been that way for a while."

Every muscle in his body prepared for the pain she'd trigger if she kept touching him. Only it never came, and he seemed to be relaxing, inch by inch under her touch. And, hell, he didn't know how that was possible. A live wire of defensiveness had been sizzling beneath his skin his entire life. And this woman had somehow worked her way around it. That was her job though, wasn't it? To figure out a system's defenses and either build it up or take it down? Tough part was, he wasn't sure which she was doing to him.

"What do you mean?" he asked. "We only got to this point because Eva was killed two months ago."

"In your world, yes. You started looking into Muñoz because you suspected he had something to do with the murder of someone you knew." She slid her hands along the back of his calf, starting from the base of his leg and working up again, and King couldn't move. Didn't want to move. "But Socorro has been focused on Sangre por Sangre for close to a year. We've been mapping out their entire organization through surveillance, financials, property records and inside intel to find their weakness. Everything we've uncovered points to a simple hierarchy with no outside influence. One man at the top with lieutenants protecting their territories across the state. Now it seems we were wrong. We're up against something much bigger than we or the Pentagon imagined, and I'm starting to think it's only a matter of time before Sangre por Sangre stops trying to hide that fact anymore."

Truth rang deep through his chest. She was right. Of course he'd carried out assignments that involved the cartel for years—a lieutenant here, a search-and-seizure there, border checks every few months—but he'd never tried to put the whole picture together before now. Before it became personal. A monster had been growing within the organization all this time and no one—not even the DEA—had suspected anything had changed. "It's Muñoz."

Scarlett lightened the pressure on his leg, the only evidence she'd heard him at all. "What do you mean?"

"He has to be the liaison between the two organizations. That's the only reason I could see him being so desperate to go after federal agents and their families to keep the triad off the DEA's radar. To come after me. He's scared."

The pieces were slowly starting to make sense, but there was still so much missing from the overall picture. Something they weren't seeing.

"He makes the connection with the triad," King said, "proposes that Sangre por Sangre can be a gateway into the United States. Only problem is, his cartel isn't the only one on the map, let alone the only one near the border. So he starts going after other organizations that can provide the same kinds of services and taking them out."

"Like the Marquez cartel. The one whose leadership was taken out in a bombing in Sangre por Sangre's warehouse ten years ago and the DEA called in Agent Roday." A brightness King had come to anticipate lit up Scarlett's eyes. She shoved to her feet as though the same kind of energy sizzling through him had transferred into her. "But why take the risk of bringing down the DEA, the ATF and Socorro on his own head? What does Muñoz get out of all of this?"

"What do lieutenants like him always want inside these organizations?" he asked.

"Power. Respect. Fear, in a lot of cases. You think he wants to be the man at the top." An audible inhale shuddered through her as she crossed the room, back and forth. "If that's the case, our intel was right. Muñoz is planning a hostile takeover from the inside. Which isn't easy. I've watched lieutenants kill each other to claw their way up that ladder, but it never works. The guy at the top isn't easily impressed. But Muñoz would have all the support he needs if he pulls off a deal moving triad product. It's a hell of a theory, but all we have to corroborate it is an empty warehouse and single fentanyl pill that was used up during testing."

"We have more than that." Though King wasn't sure how far it would take them. "Julien recognized the woman who checked him out of school the day he was abducted. Kidnapping a federal agent's son isn't something Muñoz would leave to just anyone, especially one of his soldiers. Too risky."

Scarlett stilled. "You said the only female soldier that

matched that woman's description in Muñoz's inner circle was killed a few months ago."

"There's one I hadn't considered." And he hated himself for not realizing it until now. "Though up until now, I was positive she only benefited from Muñoz's lifestyle. There's no evidence she's involved in the business."

Scarlett pointed a soft finger at him. "The wife. You think he sent his own wife to get Julien? But how... How would he have recognized her at the school unless..."

"Unless she was there the night Eva was killed." King ran through every ounce of intel he'd gathered over the past two months. None of it fit in an obvious kind of way, but he needed something—anything—he could use to get his son back. And Muñoz's wife was all he had.

"Okay." Scarlett darted to the tablet charging on her room's built-in desk. "I can work with that."

"I don't know how." Grabbing for the crutch he'd tossed on the floor last night, he wedged it beneath his arm to hike himself off the bed. "It took me a month to map out Muñoz's organization on my own, and the DEA has most likely already been by my place and seized anything pertaining to my investigation. I'm not exactly sure what you think you're going to come up with in a few minutes."

His phone fell free of his pants pocket and revealed a handful of missed calls. His supervisory special agent was most of them with a couple missed from an unknown number.

Given that the FBI had officially taken on Julien's abduction, King imagined whoever had caught the case was trying to reach out as well. The FBI didn't know Sangre por Sangre or Muñoz like King did, but damn it, he needed as much help as he could get. Covering every angle. A quick review of his voicemails assured him the FBI and local police were working the case as best they could.

But he and Scarlett were onto something here. He could feel it.

"I don't need your files. I just need…" She was lost to a series of taps and screens his brain couldn't keep up with. "Got it."

"Got what?" he asked.

"Catalina Muñoz. Forty-six. Originally born Catalina Lemos in Mexico but soon applied for citizenship once her parents immigrated into the US on a work visa when she was ten. Her parents were denied and returned to Mexico, but they left Catalina with…an uncle. Metias Leyva." Small lines creased in a half-star pattern along the edges of her eyes.

Seconds seemed to pound at the back of his head. "What is it?"

"I'm not sure yet. I feel like I should know that name." Scarlett shook her head as though to rewind the past few seconds and made a few other swipes across the screen. "Catalina managed to gain citizenship and went on to graduate with the highest marks from Columbia at the age of twenty with an MBA before marrying Hernando Muñoz a year later. No children or dependents. They own their home in Albuquerque. No work history on her part that I can see from filed joint taxes in the last seven years, but if these financials were filed right, she's never had a reason to work a day in her life."

"Where are you getting all that? Because everything you just listed requires a warrant." King tried to get a good look over her shoulder, but Scarlett pressed the tablet to her chest.

"One look at this screen, and you make yourself an accomplice. I'm pretty sure you want to keep your job with the DEA when this is over, don't you?" She eased the screen away from her chest and continued the digital flip through whatever information she'd found. "So let's just say I have my ways."

She had to be kidding, right? "Your ways? You know nothing is going to hold up in court if you can't prove you searched Muñoz's financial history legally. Even cartel lieutenants have rights."

"I'm not interested in taking Muñoz or his wife to court," she said. "All I want is to bring your son home alive. This is how I can do that, King."

The shock of her words sucker-punched him. It took him longer than it should have to get his head on straight, but he guessed that was why it was good to have a partner. Someone he could count on to keep him grounded. "I already put all this together on my own, and unless you think Catalina's background will give us an idea of where my son is being held, none of this means a damn, Scarlett."

"What if I told you I know where I heard that name? Metias Leyva. Catalina's uncle who raised her." She turned the tablet toward him and slid her finger across the screen to narrow the bird's-eye view over a property he didn't recognize. Rural, almost deserted from the look of it. "Socorro has dealt with him before."

"He's Sangre por Sangre? I mapped out Muñoz's organization during my investigation, even going as far as checking into extended family members for a lead. His name never came up in connection to Catalina," he said.

"He was Sangre por Sangre. Pretty high up, too." Scarlett set her attention back to the tablet screen. "He threw a raid party in a small town called Alpine Valley in search of his ex-wife and came up against one of our operatives. He survived the encounter, but the cartel found out he'd put his own agenda before theirs, and he couldn't face upper management without punishment. So he ran. Cops found him with a tire around his neck outside Albuquerque."

"Let me guess. Lit with accelerant and a match to make it harder to identify him. Not to mention the message it sent to the rest of the organization." King took the tablet, studying every pixel on the screen. Especially the dark rectangle positioned on a long dirt driveway. "If he's dead, then why is there an SUV parked in front of his house?"

"That's a great question." Scarlett pried open one of the doors to her built-in shelving and pressed her thumb into a safe installed inside. The keypad lit up, releasing the locking mechanism, and she handed him a sidearm. "Are you up for finding the answer?"

Chapter Twelve

The last time she ran into a suspected cartel hideout, she'd lost Gruber, Julien and almost King. This time would be different. This time she had her team. And she wasn't going to fail.

"Metias Leyva. Hell, who knew the son of a bitch would keep giving us trouble even after police had to pry that tire off what was left of him?" Granger Morais's words didn't match the gravelly voice she'd never heard raised above a warning.

The counterterrorism agent studied the property from the passenger seat of the SUV with the help of the tactical binoculars all Socorro operatives carried in their kits. Completely at ease. As though he'd done this a thousand times before. Which, she imagined, he had.

"You encounter him yourself?" King had been relegated to the back seat. More room to stretch out his leg. The plan was set in stone. He would remain behind until Scarlett and Granger cleared the property. With any luck, they'd have Julien when they returned. And if anything went south, he could call the rest of the team.

Granger lowered the binoculars and tossed them into the console between the front seats. "Not personally. No.

Though cleaning up what was left of his operation got put on me. Took a few weeks, but I managed to trace every one of his soldiers back into their dark holes or into the shallow graves where the cartel left them."

"What about Hernando Muñoz?" King asked. "The husband of Leyva's niece. Did you uncover any evidence he had something to do with Leyva's operation or have any reason to believe Muñoz was using his wife's uncle for his own agenda?"

Granger faced off with King in the rearview mirror. "None, and I dug deep. If your guy was involved in Leyva's business, they kept it off the books."

"I'm sensing a theme." Scarlett studied what she could see of the oversize mansion down the block. The DEA couldn't condone an independent investigation into the cartel led by one of their own agents. All matters concerning Hernando Muñoz would be shut down and placed under review for actionable leads, but that still left a ten-year-old boy out here on his own. The FBI didn't understand what they were dealing with. Scarlett did. She grabbed the driver side door handle. "You ready?"

"Ready as I'll ever be." Granger shoved free of the vehicle.

Scarlett craned her neck to face King. "You know the deal. You leave this vehicle only—and I mean only—if Granger and I recover Julien."

"Couldn't break out of here if I wanted to." He adjusted his weight in the seat.

A small part of her wanted to believe he'd listen to his body and not aggravate the wound. But King had proven the lengths he would go to for his son before.

"I'll be on the radio. Talk to you soon." Scarlett secured King inside the SUV, then latched the radio on to her belt and unholstered her sidearm. Sweat had already built in her hairline. "You think I should crack the window for him or something?"

Granger's laugh did nothing to release the unease building inside her as they approached the one-story mansion surrounded by nothing but desert. No cover to hide their approach. If Muñoz had a team surveilling the perimeter, they'd be made in seconds. "He's not a dog, Scarlett. The man can take care of himself."

Her unease darkened into discomfort. Her Kevlar suddenly seemed much heavier despite years of getting used to the weight. But it wasn't that. It was the feeling of something missing. Gruber and Hans, King even. In a matter of days, she'd gotten used to their team. However scattered and mismatched they were. They'd done something amazing together in that warehouse.

Scarlett looked back, putting King in her sights through the tinted window, and the pressure let up. Just for a moment. It was enough to clear her head as she turned back toward the house. The SUV was there. Right where overhead satellite footage had put it.

She and Granger jogged low, using the vehicle as cover. Scarlett pressed her hand against the SUV's window to block out the sun distorting her vision. "It's empty. Judging by the fact our footprints are the only evidence of life on this driveway, I'm guessing it's been sitting here for a couple days." Panic was starting to set in. That she'd made the wrong call. That she'd wasted another couple of hours of Julien's precious life. Of Gruber's. "Why is nobody shooting at us?"

"Your guess is as good as mine. On me." Granger raised his weapon shoulder-level and left the cover of the SUV. He and Scarlett moved as one toward the front door of the home.

Property records still put the home under Metias Leyva, the uncle. No new homeowners. Only next of kin listed was Catalina Muñoz, but this place... She didn't like how quiet it was.

It was massive. More than the two of them could search in under ten minutes. The structure sprawled out at the foot of the low-rising mountain at its back. Massive windows overlooked their position as she and Granger approached. Decorative pavers led them straight to a large overhang protecting the front door. Sunlight could barely reach into the cave-like space, and a tightness started in Scarlett's chest. Etched glass rimmed gray double doors, but no light escaped from within.

They pressed their backs into the structure on either side of the door, weapons in hand. Waiting. Her breathing was headed toward the rafters, too high to control. Granger held up three fingers, and Scarlett nodded acknowledgment.

Three. Two. One.

She put everything she had into her heel and slammed it into the space beside the dead bolt. Aged wood gave under the force, and the door slammed back on its hinges. A wall of dust rained down into Scarlett's face and collected at the back of her throat as she and Granger breached the door. This was it. This was how she made up for her mistakes.

They stepped into an oversize entryway—empty apart from a single circular table stylized with faux flowers and a stack of books. A cavern of white tile and double-story ceilings threatened to swallow them where they stood. Arches gave Scarlett a view into a sitting room off to the right decorated with ornate chairs she never would've felt comfortable sitting in. If she'd ever been invited to a cartel lieutenant's home for dinner. Over-the-top vases stuffed with dead flowers peppered the room as they followed the flow of the home.

"Something's not right here." She didn't know how else to explain it. This…knot behind her sternum. That part of her that wished she had Hans and Gruber at her side ached. She hadn't realized how much she relied on them until now. How much she needed them. "You feel that?"

"Yeah. I feel it." Granger moved into the kitchen, weapon raised high, as Scarlett pinpointed the command panel for the security system.

Holstering her weapon, she faced off with a rectangular gray cover equipped with a keyhole at the top, a camera to identify the user to the left, a card reader off to one side and a keypad with twelve digits on the other. The Ascent K2 model worked off a homeowner's cellular data with a special SIM card installed in the phone with cloud-based access from anywhere in the world. She scanned the ceiling, spotting two cameras capable of visually identifying visitors or intruders just within range. More were likely installed throughout the house and around the property, but there wasn't any indication the system was operational. The equipment wasn't affected by temperature or power outages. So why hadn't she and Granger set it off? "The system should've sent an alert the second we stepped onto the property."

"I'm guessing whoever was here didn't want to draw attention from law enforcement." Granger's even voice once again contradicted the words coming out of his mouth.

"Why do you say that?" She prodded both thumbs around the frame of the security panel, looking for a way past the keypad, keyhole, camera and card reader. Though if that were possible, this brand wouldn't be one of the top-of-the-line systems in the world.

"Because of the dead guy in the kitchen," Granger said.

Scarlett dropped her hands away from the panel, every cell in her body homed in on the pool of blood peeking out from behind the nearest kitchen cabinet at Granger's feet. Dead guy. Not dead boy. Hope expanded in her chest as she rounded into the kitchen.

And froze.

"Hernando Muñoz." Crude bandages had been wrapped around the ankle where Scarlett had sliced through the lieutenant's Achilles tendon that night in the warehouse, but that wasn't the source of all the blood. The handle of the blade dented Muñoz's chest around the wound. "Stabbed. Like Agents Roday and Dunkeld."

"Only whoever did this didn't leave a badge this time." Granger bent down, careful not to compromise the body. He pointed at one side of the bloody hole in Muñoz's chest. "There's something at the edge of the wound. Wedged in there. A business card, maybe. Hard to tell with all this blood."

"It's mine." The voice cut through her, setting every nerve ending in her body on fire.

Scarlett confronted King as he shuffled into view.

"What are you doing here? We haven't cleared the rest of the house yet, and you agreed to stay in the car until I radioed you."

"There's nobody here." Those three words shouldn't have held so much weight to them. But King was right. They would've already come into contact with Muñoz's soldiers already. King nodded at the body, his crutch offsetting the shift in his weight to the point he looked as though he'd fall at the slightest touch. "The card. It's mine."

"How can you be so sure?" Granger shoved to stand, holstering his weapon.

"Muñoz pulled it out of my pockets before tying me to a chair in his warehouse and handicapping me," King said. "Whoever did this has my son. They knew we were going to come after Muñoz, so they killed him, and now we have nothing to go on to bring Julien home."

"He's still alive, King. We're going to find him." Nervous energy shot down into Scarlett's fingertips. She needed to keep moving, keep uncovering lead after lead until she fixed this. "Granger, check the rest of the house. I need Muñoz's phone, a tablet, a laptop—anything that connects to the security system. If we're lucky, we might get something off the surveillance."

"You got it." The counterterrorism agent slipped into a parallel hallway and out of sight.

"You really think whoever did this was careless enough to leave evidence of murder behind?" King's gaze bored into her. Desperate for the answer.

"It's worth a try." Because digging through security systems and building defenses was all she knew how to do. It had to be enough. Otherwise… Julien didn't stand a chance. And that was what scared her the most. "But there is one more option. Someone I could reach out to."

King's chest and shoulders stiffened, pulling him up as straight as if a puppeteer had a hold of a string connected to the crown of his head. "What do you mean? Like a contact within Sangre por Sangre?"

"No. Not exactly. Though this person is involved in the same kind of smuggling as the cartel, and he might know where we need to look for Julien first." Her skin caught fire from the weight of his attention, but not like it had when they'd slept in the same bed together. "Before, when I told you about how I got the scar across my stomach, I didn't give you the whole story. I...couldn't."

He didn't have an answer for that, and she didn't have time to get into every detail if they wanted to recover Julien.

"The truth is my commanding officer brought me into the smuggling operation months before he tried to kill me." Her lips dried in an instant, begging for relief. Everything she'd worked to hide about her past wasn't worth the life of a child. No matter what happened next, she'd keep her word to bring Julien home. "I saw him do things I wasn't supposed to in that time, and I think I can use it to get him to help us."

HE COULDN'T BREATHE. Couldn't think.

"Wait. You..." King tried to get his head around what she was trying to tell him while also trying to ignore the dead body at her feet. "He brought you in before the night you were stabbed and left for dead? Which means, you were in on the smuggling operation from the beginning."

"Yes. I was one of the soldiers stealing cash, weapons and drugs the army confiscated from the enemy forces in the area." Her voice cracked. As though she'd never admitted any of this out loud. And given the fact she wasn't sitting somewhere in a cell that didn't exist on paper, King put his money on the idea she hadn't. "My commanding officer believed my skills for security systems and defense could work in their favor. And he was right. I made sure none of us were caught."

Scarlett took a step forward but stopped her approach as every muscle around King's spine hardened with battle-ready tension. "King, I give you my word, I thought we were putting those resources to good use. I didn't know the full extent of what they were doing, and I needed—"

"What did you need, Scarlett? The drugs? The money?" The answer didn't matter. Blood drained from his upper body in a rush, nearly knocking him over. The woman standing in front of him wasn't the one he'd partnered with over the past few days, the one who'd given him her word to bring his son home.

"No. I just…" Her gaze cut somewhere past his left arm. "I thought we were doing something good. They told me everything was going back to the people we were trying to help, but it was a lie." A glimmer of tears reflected in her eyes. "Two weeks before I ended up in that hospital, I found out about the human trafficking. My CO and the rest of my team were selling off women and kids to the highest bidders, and I pulled out. I made a plan to expose the entire operation, but I made a mistake. I trusted the wrong person. That's when my commanding officer decided I couldn't walk away alive."

"And what? You want to get in contact with him and ask for help to find my son?" King tried to thread his hand through his hair, for something to distract him from the churn of rage and betrayal, but his balance shot to one side. "No. You know what? Don't answer that. Because you're just digging yourself deeper. I have grounds to arrest you and hand you over to the army, Scarlett."

"Not as long as you're suspended from the DEA, you don't." She took another step, her voice softening, but it wouldn't work. The manipulation, her proximity—none of it would affect him. Not anymore.

"You lied to me." And that was what hurt the most, wasn't it? That Eva had lied about his son's existence for ten years. That Adam had lied about running his own investigation into Sangre por Sangre while preaching they had to work by the book. But of all the people he'd trusted to have his back, Scarlett was supposed to be different. A partner. Someone who didn't break their ideals and proceeded on logic and truth. Someone he could rely on to bring his son home.

Only that hadn't been the case at all. He never knew that person.

That was all anyone was. Appearances.

And he'd taken them all at face value.

"King, listen to me. Hernando Muñoz is dead. The man who orchestrated Julien's abduction is dead and so is any reason or personal revenge he had to do it. Muñoz had leverage by keeping Julien alive, which gave us time to strategize until he made his move." Her breathing picked up, making her words wispier. Urgent. "Whoever killed Muñoz has your son. Only now they have no use for Julien. They'll use him until he doesn't serve a purpose, and it already might be too late, but I can help. I can reach out to my former CO with where to start looking. I gave you my word—"

"What does your word mean, Scarlett?" The cavern of emptiness he'd tried to fill with his job ached around the edges. For the first time in…ever, he'd finally felt as though he was on the right path. Becoming a father, claiming justice for Eva and Adam, trusting Socorro with Julien's life. But it'd all been a lie. "You just admitted to being an active participant in an international smuggling ring during your service. Anything you've said up until now has been corrupted. Your word means nothing to me. You mean nothing to me, and as of this moment, we're done."

He regretted the words the instant he said them, but there it was. Seeping into the silence between them.

Her mouth parted, and a vulnerability he hadn't witnessed escaped on her next exhale. Color drained from her face and neck, and King half expected her to collapse, but in an instant that raw part of her was contained. As though it never existed. That guarded armor he'd managed to crack through the past few days returned, agonizing second by second, until King couldn't read anything in her expression.

Scarlett shifted her weight center, almost a full inch taller as she faced off with him. "Well, I'm glad we cleared that up. Consider your deal with Socorro void, Agent Elsher. Should the DEA require statements as to your investigation in Hernando Muñoz from our operatives, please have them reach out to Granger Morais. He'll be happy to assist."

Agent Elsher. Not King. The formality stabbed through

him as effectively as the blade in his thigh and sent an earthquake of renewed pain into his nervous system. But King wouldn't break. Not as long as Julien was still out there.

"House is clear. No signs of clothing or toiletries left behind. Whoever was here didn't stay long. Must've taken Muñoz's devices, too." Granger rounded back into the kitchen and stopped dead cold. With palpable tension, his hand eased toward the sidearm at his hip as the counterterrorism agent's gaze bounced between King and his teammate. "Everything okay?"

"We're done here." King's own words seemed to hit harder when coming from Scarlett's mouth. She tried for a smile, but everyone in the room saw the forced nature behind it. "We can call the body into Albuquerque PD from the SUV. Agent Elsher is going to babysit the scene until they arrive."

King hadn't volunteered. But without Socorro resources, staying behind would give him the chance to search the place himself before police arrived on the scene. There had to be something here that could tell him where Julien was. It was Locard's principle. Anyone coming onto a crime scene left a piece of themselves behind, and anyone leaving took pieces with them. No matter how small. "I just want to find my son."

He sounded hollow. Way too calm and casual about the fact she was about to walk out that door and out of his life forever. Possibly taking the only chance Julien had with her.

"So do I." Scarlett gave a final nod before maneuvering around him. Her boots echoed off the fancy tile until the pitch changed, and King couldn't hear her or Granger's steps.

He was thrown into a silence punctuated only by his own thoughts.

King forced his weight onto his good leg and took a step forward. The island with the body on the other side of it spanned the length of the entire kitchen and didn't leave a whole lot of room for an injured former DEA agent with a bad leg to navigate.

His heart seemed a whole hell of a lot heavier than it had a minute ago as he caught Socorro's SUV pulling away from the house. Albuquerque PD would arrive to investigate the body. He had ten, maybe fifteen minutes before he'd be forced to take a back seat. He needed something now.

King set the crutch against the counter, not caring when the damn thing slid out of reach and hit the tile with a metallic bounce. His good knee collapsed onto the cream tile, and it took everything he had not to fall onto the body while trying to hold himself together.

Moving or searching a body before the medical examiner had a chance to catalogue the remains wouldn't help his case with the DEA, but King couldn't wait. Because Scarlett was right about one thing. They were already out of time. Julien was out there. Without anyone to look after him or use him for their own agenda. Alone. Scared. Possibly hurt.

"Come on, Muñoz. You gotta give me something. Where would you have stashed a ten-year-old kid?"

King plucked at the blood-soaked business card stabbed into the bastard's wound. Why the hell had Muñoz hung on to it? The son of the bitch had his son.

Having King's contact information wouldn't have done him a damn bit of good.

King memorized the bruising settling at the back of the lieutenant's neck. Tortured. Thoroughly. And for an extended period of time. But that didn't make sense. Muñoz served the cartel. Why kill him with his own MO unless…

Acid surged up his throat as he pieced the business card back together. Muñoz's blood raced into the whorls and loops of his fingerprints. The front looked like every other business card King handed out to witnesses, victims and sources. Apart from one element. His first name had been circled in smeared dark ink.

Turning the card over, King stared at the scrawled handwriting across the back. Recognition iced through him as he read the phone number over and over. Not in his handwriting, but Adam's.

He cut his attention to Muñoz's face, trying to come up with why his former partner would've had any motive to reach out to Muñoz one on one. Close enough to hand the lieutenant one of King's business cards. And only came up with a single answer. "Son of a bitch. You were helping them, weren't you? You were Adam and Eva's source."

Muñoz had wanted the DEA to breach the warehouse. Had given Adam and Eva what they needed to investigate. Which meant Muñoz hadn't ordered Eva's murder or had anything to do with Adam's death. Someone else had. Someone who'd caught onto Muñoz's betrayal and killed him for it.

That was why the lieutenant had been so desperate for King to hand over Eva and Adam's investigation files. He'd needed something from them. A way out of the cartel? A chance to get away from someone within? Then he'd used Julien to try to force King's hand.

Only Scarlett and King hadn't been able to break the cipher Adam and Eva used to manually encrypt their notes, and Muñoz wasn't talking anymore. King had nothing to support his theory, but the pieces fit the violent and bloody puzzle scattered around him.

He stared at the inked circle around his name.

"It can't be that easy." His name. It was the four-letter word that linked them all together, wasn't it? Except now the DEA had the physical case files, and King had left the copies with Scarlett. It would take a court order for her to hand it over after the way they'd left things.

Pounding footsteps charged his defenses into overdrive, and King used the edge of the counter to bring himself to his feet.

"Police! Is anyone here?" Two officers penetrated his vision, weapons aimed. At him. "Sir, I'm going to need you to step away from the body with your hands up."

"Agent Elsher, DEA." One hand raised in surrender, King dragged his badge from beneath his shirt for the officers to inspect for themselves. "I know this is bad timing, but I'm going to need a ride."

Chapter Thirteen

Her heart hurt.

It wasn't the shame of her past that pinned her to the back of the seat. It was King. His parting words circled her brain until they blurred together in one long streak. She'd meant nothing to him. After everything they'd been through together. After risking her own life—and the lives of her K9s—for him. She was nothing but something to be used for his own gain.

Just as she had been for her former commanding officer.

"You want to tell me what happened back there?" Granger slid his palms along the steering wheel's frame as he checked the driver side mirror. "Last I checked, Elsher is the one who brought us into this mess."

Scarlett forced her gaze out the window as the tears burned. Dirt kicked up alongside the SUV and pinged off the metal frame as they carved through the desert. The suspension failed to absorb every bump in the road, knocking them around in their seats, but the internal beating was so much worse. "I told him the truth. About what happened overseas."

"How much of the truth?" A small inflection in his

voice was the only evidence Granger Morais had an opinion about any of this. It warned her to choose her words very carefully. Because what she'd done on tour didn't just involve her. Her teammate could be brought up on conspiracy charges for hauling her off base to that hospital if the army identified him.

"All of it." She saw the mistake now. Trusting a federal agent with information that could put her behind bars for the rest of her life. "He didn't take it well, and I don't know what he's going to do now."

"Damn it, Scarlett." Granger's disappointment burrowed beneath the hurt and the invisible pain suffocating her second by second, stealing the last of any remaining self-compassion she had. "We had a deal. I risked everything to save your life, and the only thing I asked in return was for you to keep the details of your involvement in the smuggling ring between us. You're less than a year from your discharge. The army can still court-martial you. They can come after us both."

"I know. I'm sorry. I just… I wanted to fix this." She didn't know what else to say, what to think. Tears escaped her control. Humiliating and hot and uncomfortable. She swiped at her face to get rid of the evidence of her grief and triggered the underlying pain of her broken nose.

This wasn't her. She was the one who was supposed to keep Socorro safe. She was the one who held it together for the sake of everyone else on the team. That was her job. To remain logical and strong and perfect so as to keep the people she cared about alive. But she wasn't any of that. Hadn't been for a long time.

Had she ever?

"Muñoz was the only one keeping King's son alive. With him dead, there's no telling what the cartel will do with a ten-year-old kid. My gut is telling me they'll sell him as soon as they get the chance. I thought if I could reach out to my former CO—"

Granger slammed on the brakes, and the SUV jolted forward.

She threw her palms out first to keep herself from hitting the dashboard as the entire vehicle groaned to a stop.

"Tell me you didn't." The counterterrorism agent faced off with her from the driver's seat. "Tell me you didn't put us both at risk for a DEA agent you've only known for three days."

Her stomach felt as though it'd shot up into her throat as the dust settled around them. Three days. Was that really all it had taken for King to convince her the past couldn't hold her back anymore? That she could make up for all the wrong stacked against her by bringing a little boy home to his dad and solving a case he so desperately needed to end? That she was good enough?

Didn't seem like any time at all, and in the same moment, an entire lifetime. Of her prodding him with jokes and getting a glimpse of that off-center smile in return. Of his hands on her waist as she dared to reveal the darkest parts of her soul. Three days had slipped through her fingers and into the void. She'd wanted more. So much more.

Mornings of waking up to him in her bed. Foot massages after hard days. The scent of him filling her lungs. King watching her back in the field. Him. It was all him. The one man who'd convinced her she could be the good in the world. Gravity suctioned her deeper into the seat and stole the air from her lungs. She hadn't just left King back at that crime scene. She'd left her heart, and she wasn't sure she could ever get it back. "No. You're safe. I'm the only one who's at risk. And if the army court-martials me, I'll make sure your name never comes up."

"That doesn't make me feel any better." Pulling onto the road, Granger pushed the SUV through a dip and maneuvered them back on track. The hum of the engine and crunch of rock under the tires settled between them. "You want to know why I pulled you out of that hanger after your CO tried to gut you?"

"It wasn't out of the goodness of your heart?" She'd meant it as a joke, a way to get rid of the heaviness constricting her chest, but the memories were there. Just waiting for her to give them the attention she'd fought against for close to a year. It'd been easier the past few days. Believing once she and King brought Julien home that she'd never have to think about them again.

"I clocked your operation while running my assignment for Socorro. I knew you and your crew were skimming from the resources the rangers confiscated from the other side." Socorro's headquarters—tucked back into the mountains with gleaming sharp black lines—came into view, and Granger hit the overhead button to signal the gate. The crowd of picketers had thinned over the past few days, but the ones left swarmed the gate with their neon signs and harsh words. No sign of added security though. Ivy must've decided a few protestors weren't worth the extra effort. "And I followed you that night so I could use you to lead me to the others. It worked."

Surprise pulled her attention from one of the protestors. A man wearing a thick coat in the middle of the desert. All this time, she'd imagined Granger Morais as the knight in Kevlar who just happened to come across her broken body and save her life. Not the one who could've put an end to it. "You could've turned me in. Why didn't you?"

"Because of all the moving pieces in the smuggling operation, you were the only one who was doing what your CO told you everyone else was." He locked that crystal clear blue-green gaze on her as the SUV dipped into the underground parking garage. "You were the one giving back what you took to the people in the region who needed it. Yeah, you were stealing cash and guns and drugs, but that money made it into the hands of women having a hard time feeding their kids and to organizations who were trying to help conditions in the villages."

Her throat threatened to close in on itself.

"I heard you that night. Telling your CO you were going to expose them for the human trafficking." Her teammate pulled the SUV into his assigned spot and cut the engine. Only he didn't move. Shadows carved across his face, like he was some kind of villain trying to hide in the dark. "I saw the knife. I still remember the sound of it cutting into you. How you seemed so surprised. And I knew right then what kind of person you were."

Pain flared through her midsection, and a rush of nausea pushed up into her throat. "What kind of person am I?"

"Broken." That single word punctured through the pounding in her head, aggravated by the evenness of Granger's voice. "Like the rest of us. The only difference is you don't want to accept that being broken is what makes you stronger than anyone else on this team. You put everyone's needs ahead of your own for that exact reason. Because you don't want them to end up broken like you."

"It's still not enough." Her lungs felt too tight. Like they'd somehow overfilled and emptied at the same time. "No matter what I do—how hard I try—it doesn't work. I'm still the woman that got conned into believing I was making a difference."

"That's the woman I recommended for this job, Scarlett," Granger said. "The one who fought to fix her mistake. And I know for a fact that's who Agent Elsher believes in—"

An explosion rocked through the entire garage.

"Get down!" Scarlett brought her hands to her head as though she could stop the entire parking garage from coming down on top of them. Debris slammed against her side of the vehicle and cracked the bulletproof glass. A tingling sensation swept from crown to toe as cement dust cleared.

Shouts penetrated the SUV's glass as she watched the armored garage gate hit the floor. She unholstered her weapon. "We're under attack. I can't see how many, but they brought more than guns."

"Get to the elevator." Granger pulled his weapon, keeping his head well below the window. "I'll hold them off as long as I can and get them away from the civilians."

"I'm not leaving you down here alone." Trying to gauge the manpower waiting outside the vehicle was useless. There was too much debris. "You have no idea how many of them are out there."

"Yes, you are. You're the only one who knows how to trigger the building's backup defense system." Granger shouldered his door open and motioned her over his lap. "Go. Now."

The structure's alarms pierced through the garage. Red lights circled in distress to inform the entire team they were under attack. "You better be alive at the end of this."

"Ditto. Now get out of here before this place collapses on itself." Granger backed out of the driver seat, using the SUV as cover to get a count of how many attackers waited at the entrance.

She followed his retreat. Only she kept moving, past the back of the vehicle, weaving between the SUVs parked between her and the elevator. A light outline stood out against the black backdrop. She was almost there.

Gunshots popped in succession. A bullet whizzed past her ear, and Scarlett lunged for the keypad as Granger returned fire. A groan broke through the drone of lead. She punched in her security code and turned to face the onslaught of the attack as the elevator doors took their time. Weapon raised, she caught sight of movement to her left and took aim. She compressed the trigger. The gun kicked back in her hand a split second after the round found its mark. The man she'd noted outside, dressed in a coat. The cartel was among the protestors. Using them as cover. Damn it. The attackers were inside, maneuvering behind Granger's position. One wrong move, and she'd lose a member of her team.

The elevator announced its arrival.

Two more shots. Another moan of pain.

"Move it, Beam!" Granger retreated behind his vehicle and repositioned. He fired another round of shots. "Get out of here!"

Scarlett stepped backward into the elevator against her heart's will. He was right. She was the only one who could put a stop to this attack before it had a chance to reach the others. The doors started to close.

Just as Granger took a bullet and hit the ground.

KING HAD THE CIPHER. Now he just needed Eva and Adam's notes to test his theory about Muñoz's involvement in the case.

Except smoke was spiraling up from Socorro's headquarters a mile out. Black and wispy. Like the place was on fire.

"Step on it." King held on to the dashboard and the passenger side door as the Albuquerque PD officer hit the accelerator. His heart rate rocketed to dangerous levels as the last curve onto the one-lane dirt road gave him a straight view of the building. "Call for backup. Albuquerque, Alpine Valley. Everyone. Socorro Security is under attack."

The officer detached the radio from the dash and called in the orders to any available officers in the vicinity as King mapped out the source of the damage.

"Head for the garage." He pointed to the west side of the structure, automatically leaning forward as though he could somehow make the patrol vehicle go faster.

"Sir, we need to wait for backup and fire and rescue. There's no telling what we're walking into," the officer said.

"Then wait, but I'm going in there." His leg be damned.

There was only one organization stupid enough and with enough resources to attack a private military contractor like Socorro. The cartel wanted whatever intel Muñoz had given up to the DEA and ATF. They wanted the case file King had left in Scarlett's possession.

His ass left the seat as the patrol car throttled over the uneven landscape. Unholstering his weapon, King released the magazine and counted the ammunition inside. Hell, he'd gone through it all while trying to give Scarlett and Julien an escape in the warehouse, and he hadn't slowed down long enough to restock. He couldn't go in there without a weapon.

"Drop me here. Wait for backup and tell whoever's in charge that Sangre por Sangre is inside, armed and highly dangerous. Oh, and if you have any extra 9mm Luger ammunition, that would be greatly appreciated."

The car skidded to a stop, threatening to throw him through the windshield, but King didn't have time for any other injuries. Scarlett was in there. He had to go. King kicked the passenger side door open. He reached back in and threw a thank-you to the officer who handed him a box of fresh ammunition. "Reach out to the supervisory special agent of the DEA in Albuquerque. Tell him Agent Elsher is on the scene. He'll know what to do."

King slammed the door behind him, effectively putting an end to any change of mind. He packed the magazine of his weapon and jammed the heavy metal casing into place. Intense desert heat beaded sweat at the back of his neck, but it was nothing compared to the heat coming off the building. Flames licked at the garage entrance he and Scarlett had slid beneath two days ago.

She'd spent her entire career with Socorro building defenses against attacks on this place. He wasn't going to be able to walk through the front door.

He had to go straight into the belly of the beast.

King tested his weight on his bad leg and regretted the choice immediately. But there was no other option. No other way for him to get inside. And he had to. He had to get to Scarlett.

She was the only reason he was standing here.

The past three days had blurred into a chaotic stream of bullets and blood and loss, but all the while, she'd been the one to keep him grounded. Their ridiculous debates and jabs at one another had kept him from spiraling. For the first time in years, someone had made him laugh, but it was her determination to leave the world better than how she'd found it that had convinced him she could bring Julien home.

And he wasn't letting her go. Not yet.

Scarlett's personal mission to make up for the past by giving her all—including her own life—for a kid she hadn't even met outweighed everything she'd told him about her involvement in the smuggling ring overseas. And he'd been an idiot to think a single cell in her beautiful body could be corrupted so easily. That she could hurt anyone.

All she'd done was prove over and over again that he needed her. Back in the warehouse. In this case. In his life. And, damn it, he wasn't ready to give that up.

Because he loved her.

In a matter of days, Scarlett had broken through the wall he'd built around him and Julien over the past two months and given him something to look forward to. A reason to keep going.

"I'm coming. Just hang on a bit longer." King added weight to his leg and took that first step toward the garage. Adrenaline raced to block the pain in his nerves, but it wouldn't be enough. The stitches around his wound screamed for his crutch. No. He could do this. He had to do this. His heel caught on a rock and worked to tip him off balance, but he was stronger now. Because of Julien. Because of Scarlett. Everything they'd been through had led him to this moment.

A gunshot echoed from the garage entrance.

He took a second step. Then another. His body adapted to the barbed wire curling through his thigh muscle, and he picked up the pace. He had no idea what he was walking into, but it didn't matter. His future was in that building, and he wasn't going to turn his back on it anymore. They were going to get through this. Together.

Two SUVs angled inward on either side of the entrance ahead.

King took position behind the one on the left, scanning the interior for movement. Instead, he found an arsenal. "Don't mind if I do."

Grabbing for the hatch release, he let the cargo door swing upward on its hydraulics and exposed an entire selection of automatic weapons, grenades and ammunition. He tucked a flash grenade in each pocket, cutting his gaze around the vehicle to keep an eye out for anyone left standing guard. Then grabbed for the nearest rifle. "I'll just ignore the fact it's illegal to drive around with all this."

Leaving the cargo area open, King maneuvered to the front of the SUV along the driver's side. Fire raged mere feet from the bumper and flashed hot along the exposed skin of his arms, face and neck. The longer the flames burned, the more unstable the building would get. He couldn't wait for fire and rescue. He had to go now. "It's just a couple arm hairs. They'll grow back."

King took two deep breaths, then held the third. And took the leap.

He hauled himself over the threshold of the entrance, barely missing the reach of flames. Colliding with a wall of human muscle on the other side.

The cartel soldier stumbled forward and slammed into another SUV parked a few feet ahead. King tried to get his strength back into his legs, but the added gear was holding him down. He dropped the assault rifle as the soldier turned on him.

A fist connected with the left side of his face and sent King spiraling toward the cement. Fire licked at the back of his neck. He rolled to avoid the flames and took out the soldier's legs in the process. The two-hundred-pound attacker landed directly on top of him, shoving the air from his chest.

King grabbed for one of the grenades stashed in his pants pocket, pulled the pin and shoved it between the soldier's Kevlar and rib cage. He kicked the son of a bitch out of reach and, plugging his ears, he scrambled out of the blast radius as fast as his leg allowed.

A panicked scream was cut short as the device exploded.

Smoke drove into King's lungs as he forced himself

to his feet. He collected the assault rifle and set the butt of the weapon into his shoulder. "Who's next?"

A gunshot burst from his right, and King turned the rifle on the shooter. His bullets cut through the thick smoke pouring down from the garage ceiling.

Something heavy hit the ground. No more gunshots.

King kept moving, working his way through the maze of parked vehicles. The elevator access into the building had to be close. He pressed forward, putting everything he had into staying on his feet. He rounded the final vehicle.

And faced off with a gun pointed directly at him.

Granger Morais's hands bobbed with every exaggerated breath. One second. Two. The counterterrorism agent seemed to think better of pulling the trigger and let his arms collapse into his chest. Lying back, Granger stared up at the ceiling. "Where the hell did you come from?"

"Outside." King noted the dark puddle of liquid pooling beneath the operative's right side and took another step forward. "You don't look so good."

"You think I'll be ready for my date later tonight?" A half scoff, half laugh seemed to aggravate whatever wound Granger had sustained in his shoulder. Pain contorted his expression and tightened the muscles along his arms. "It's just a scratch. She won't notice, right?"

"You might want to reschedule. Or, hey, hospital food isn't as bad as everyone thinks. It's not every day you get to visit a cafeteria. She'll certainly remember it." King swung the rifle to his back, the strap digging into his shoulder. He offered Granger a hand. "What happened here?"

Granger didn't hesitate and slid a calloused palm into King's. A groan escaped the operative's control as King hauled him to his feet. "They blew through the gate. My guess is with C-4. Never saw them coming."

Dread pooled at the base of King's spine as he scoured what he could see of the garage. Wide cracks splintered across the ceiling. The weight of this entire building could drop right on them without warning. They had to get everyone out of here. "Where is Scarlett?"

"I sent her upstairs. We needed her to call the shots." Granger rolled his shoulder back, pulling a scream from his chest a split second before he doubled over. Not even the most experienced operators could outrun a bullet.

"Have you heard from her since?" They got to the elevator, and King swept the area one last time as Granger set his key card against the reader. Seconds ticked by— slower than he wanted.

"I kind of had other things on my mind." The counterterrorism agent collapsed against the wall near the key card panel. "Not dying, for one."

Movement registered from the crumbling gate.

An armored vehicle tore through the mess and rammed into the first two SUVs in its way. The crash threatened to trigger an avalanche of steel, cement and wood and bring the entire building down on top of them.

King checked the elevator's progress, swinging the rifle into both hands. "We've got company."

"We already had company," Granger said.

The elevator pinged before opening its doors. King fisted the operative's shirt and dragged him inside the car as an army of cartel soldiers spilled out of the armored truck. "That was just the first wave."

Chapter Fourteen

Her feet slipped out from under her. Scarlett hit the clean black tile with a thud. Oxygen stretched out of reach the harder she tried to control the impact. Her fingernails clawed into the thin grout, but it was no use getting to her feet.

Alarms screeched from every hallway. Socorro was under attack. Whoever blew through the gate had tripped the system. Any operatives inside would already be taking battle positions. Cash and Jocelyn on the roof with their high-powered rifles, Jones armed with his personal arsenal on the elevators and Granger… She'd left him in the garage. Watched him take a bullet.

But she couldn't think about that right now.

Her job was easy. Get to the security room. That was where she could do the most damage. Scarlett shoved to her feet. The aches and bruises from the past few days wouldn't slow her down. She wouldn't let them. She dug her toes into the floor to propel her forward. Right, then two lefts. She collided with the door that prevented anyone but her and Ivy Bardot access to the security room and scrambled for her key card.

Every second counted on the battlefield. One wrong

move. That was all it would take, and she and her team would lose everything.

Scarlett nearly fell over the threshold as the door released. Loud voices punctured through the radio sitting in its charging station on the desk. An entire array of monitors cast a blue-white glow across the darkened room. Cameras covered every angle of the structure, and Scarlett worked to get eyes on the rest of her team. She grabbed for the earpiece left in its power cradle.

"Gotham and I are in position on level two." Jones's voice was staticky in her ear. "Anyone manages to get inside, they won't make it far."

"Hold your position. Scarlett, shut down the elevators. We're not going to make it easy for them." She imagined Ivy Bardot secured in her office, armed, with both eyes on the surveillance.

"Granger's in the garage trying to hold them back," Scarlett said. "That's his only way out."

Thousands of possibilities screamed for attention at the back of her mind, but only one stood out. Sangre por Sangre. Scarlett scanned the multitude of monitors for her teammate, but there was something else in the garage. Something that shouldn't be there. Her skin tightened to the point she was convinced her bones would crumble to dust inside her own body. "Be advised, hostiles have brought in an armored vehicle. I count fifteen—no, sixteen—armed enemy combatants in the garage, but I don't see Granger."

"Damn it. Get eyes on him. Now." Ivy's voice notched an octave higher.

Socorro had never been attacked in its own territory. For as many years of experience each of Ivy's operatives had gathered, this was a first for all of them outside of their military careers. And it was showing. "Cash, Jocelyn. I need you on that roof in case more are on their way. Where the hell are you?"

"Almost there." Socorro's forward observer—Cash Meyers—sounded out of breath. "Do you know how many stairs there are in this place? Not to mention how much gear I'm carrying."

"Just keep climbing. Just keep climbing." Logistics coordinator Jocelyn Carville sang her own personal mantra.

"I will end you." Cash's threat meant nothing when an entire drug cartel had breached their home base.

"Has anyone contacted Dr. Piel or the veterinarian?" Jones Driscoll looked up into the camera set on him. "Might be a good time to let them know to stay in their offices."

"On it." Scarlett took out her cell and tapped out the message to both physicians. An instant reply buzzed through from the vet.

Hans ran when the alarms went off.

"What?" The question was more for herself as Scarlett instructed the vet to shelter in place. Her female K9 was missing with the other one unaccounted for after the fight at the warehouse. In a matter of hours, she'd lost everything she held dear. She wasn't sure she could take much more.

"I've got movement on the elevator." Jones hiked his rifle into his shoulder on the monitor, but all Scarlett could see was a bunch of blurred pixels as her world unraveled right before her eyes.

"Scarlett, where is Granger?" Ivy's voice tried to keep her in the present, but grief and a stabbing of fear kept her from engaging in the moment. "Scarlett?"

She tossed her phone on the desk. Tears prickled at her eyes, but she couldn't focus on that right now. Her mind was being pulled in a thousand different directions, and she couldn't make sense of a single one of them. She scoured the monitors. Hans had to still be in the building, and there was nothing Scarlett could do about it.

"Uh, guys. Elevator. On the move." Jones backed up a step, ready to engage anyone who came through the elevator doors.

"Working on it." Scarlett ran through the elevator protocol as fast as her fingers allowed and found the line of code to take the system offline. "There."

The elevator's LED panel froze on the screen. Whoever was hoping to get onto the level would be stuck until Scarlett deemed otherwise.

"Wait. I hear something from inside." Jones took a hesitant step forward. The combat controller let his weapon swing free as he pressed one side of his head to the doors on the screen. "Oh, hell. It's Granger. Bring the elevator back up."

Her heart jump-started at the news. Granger was alive. "I shut the whole system down. It's going to take at least two minutes to bring it back online."

Two minutes Granger might not have.

"We don't have that kind of time." Jocelyn's voice was no longer singsongy. "I've got five more vehicles headed our way. Cartel based off the makes and models. No telling how many more soldiers inside. A half mile out."

"I've got another dust cloud coming in from the east," Cash said. "Can't be sure who it is yet."

"They're cutting off any chance of escape." Ivy went silent for a series of seconds, every single one of them waiting for the next order. "Scarlett, I need you to get the secondary system ready."

Shock stole Scarlett's confidence to win this battle. "Are you sure?"

"This firm is a direct connection to the Pentagon and every other federal organization we've partnered with to undermine Sangre por Sangre." Socorro's founder didn't wait for an answer. "If the cartel gets their hands on any of the intel we've used, they'll be able to identify our inside source, and there will be no stopping them, and that is something none of us can come back from. Get the system ready."

Jones let his rifle drop to his side as he threaded his fingers between the elevator doors. Muscles Scarlett would never have in her life flexed as he tried to pry the doors open by hand. "Why does that sound like we're launching a nuclear missile?" he asked.

"Because that's basically what we'll be doing." Scarlett brought up the program she'd built from the ground up. One press of the button. That was all it would take to appease Socorro's enemies and ensure the team never interrupted cartel operations again. Because none of them would make it out of here alive. A chain reaction of fear and determination and grief knotted her nerves. "The entire building will be demolished."

"Whoa. What the hell are you talking about?" Wind caught Cash's last word from the roof and made it difficult to hear through the earpiece. "What is the secondary defense system?"

Scarlett took a deep breath as a flood of cartel members spread through the garage. They searched every SUV and confiscated individual weapons from the back of each vehicle. She let her hand slip to her sidearm, hoping beyond hope it would be enough. "C-4. Wired over every square inch of this place."

"It's not every day you get a front row seat to the end of the world, but at least we're all together." Jocelyn's voice cracked a split second before a dog bark pierced the open channel. Her German shepherd, Maverick, had been the logistic coordinator's partner as long as Scarlett could remember. "I'm going silent. I need to call Baker."

The green LED connected to Jocelyn's earpiece on Scarlett's monitor went red as her teammate reached out to her life partner, Alpine Valley's chief of police.

"Got it!" Jones pried the elevator doors apart and leveraged one leg into the gap to keep it from closing.

Granger slapped a hand onto the tile and hauled himself free of the elevator that wasn't quite level with the floor yet. Only he wasn't alone.

The desk bit into her sore midsection as Scarlett tried to get a better view of the man following the counterterrorism agent, but her instincts had already put two and two together. Her nails bit into her palms as she recognized the sharp jawline and dirty blond hair. "King."

She pushed away from the desk to intercept him but caught another range of movement on a monitor. One of the armored vehicles. An outline of white in the middle of so much darkness and destruction.

A woman stepped down from the back of the vehicle.

So out of place. Long dark hair lay in tendrils past her shoulders and framed a heart-shaped face. Her white blazer and pant set put her in a whole other category of wealth and security as the soldiers around her fanned out.

Catalina Muñoz.

"It's her." Scarlett wasn't sure who she was talking to, but the comms were still open. "Catalina Muñoz. She's here. This is all happening because of her."

"Who the hell is Catalina Muñoz?" Jones's question seemed to catch King's attention on the monitor.

"Who are you talking to?" The DEA agent fought her teammate for his earpiece and won out, shoving the device into his own ear. "Who is this?"

Their last conversation—his accusations—undermined everything she knew about herself and her ability to get her team out of here alive. "Agent Elsher."

"Scarlett." King searched the corridor until he found the nearest camera and limped toward it, his gaze searing straight through the monitor. "I put it all together. Hernando Muñoz was a source. Adam and Eva were using him to get to the triad. If Catalina's here, that means she's the one who killed him. She's the real brains behind the operation. Taking out the other cartels, partnering with the triad, abducting Julien. It's all because of her. Where is she?"

Scarlett turned her attention back to the monitor overlooking the inside of Socorro's garage. Instantly on high alert as Catalina stared into the camera lens. "In the garage."

Catalina turned toward someone or something still in the truck before facing off with the surveillance. Another pixelated outline—smaller—appeared on the screen. And then Julien came into view.

"King," she said. "She has your son."

KING DISLODGED THE EARPIECE.

"King! There are more on the way!" Scarlett's voice crackled just before he handed the device back to the operative in front of him.

Pointing to Granger, King backed toward the elevator car still uneven with the floor. "You're going to want to get him to a doctor."

"There's no way out of here that doesn't put you in their sights, Elsher." Granger's usually frustratingly even voice dipped as he latched on to his shoulder. "They'll kill you the second they get eyes on you."

"Not before I kill them first." King's gaze caught the surveillance camera. He knew Scarlett was watching, and he got as close to it as he could. He didn't know whether or not they had sound or if she could make out his words, but it didn't matter. He had to tell her. That he was wrong, that she meant something to him, that she was everything he'd tried to avoid in his life and everything he needed at the same time.

"I love you." There wasn't any more he could say.

King turned his back on the camera—on whatever future they might've had—and headed for the elevator door. He set the rifle against his chest, ready for whatever waited on the other side. Because it was the only way to get to his son. And save the woman he loved. If he could slow Sangre por Sangre down, there was a chance the entire Socorro team could live to fight another day.

Only one way to find out.

"You really think you're going to survive whatever is down there without a vest?" The operative King hadn't met before—the one who had forced open the elevator doors for them—stripped the Velcro from the side of his ribs and pulled his Kevlar vest over his head. Offering it with one hand, he hiked Granger's arm around his shoulder for support with the other. "Thought you DEA types were smarter than that."

"You'd be surprised." King hauled the rifle strap over his head, took the vest and slipped into it before replacing the weapon. There were more on the way. That was the last thing he'd heard Scarlett say. The cartel had most likely surrounded the place, cutting off any chance of escape. Socorro operatives would have to prioritize, Scarlett included, leaving him to fight this particular battle alone. "Thanks."

Electricity powered up behind him, and the elevator car closed the distance to the last level. Scarlett. With a half salute toward the camera, he smiled. "Wish me luck."

King stepped into the elevator, facing off with his own reflection as the doors closed down the middle. Gravity suctioned his stomach into the bottom of his torso as the floors counted off on the LED panel overhead. "I'm going to need it."

The elevator pinged just before a thud registered from under his feet as the car landed on the garage level. One second. Two.

The doors parted.

Smoke and dust and diesel infiltrated his senses as King stepped out. A circle of soldiers took aim, and he raised his hands in surrender. "I come in peace."

"I'm not entirely sure that's true, Agent Elsher." The semicircle parted down the middle, exposing the source of the voice. Catalina Muñoz, in the flesh. "I seem to recall having to clean up quite a few bodies at my warehouse two days ago. You wouldn't believe how hard it is to get blood out of cement."

He wasn't going to apologize for that. He wasn't going to apologize for anything concerning this investigation. "Where is my son?"

"Right here." Catalina half turned and reached behind her. Long fingers wrapped around the back of his son's neck and drew him forward away from the soldier guarding the ten-year-old. "Julien has done a fine job of keeping me company, haven't you, dear?"

"I'm here, buddy." Every cell in King's body wanted to rip Julien out of Catalina's grasp, but that would surely get him a few bullet holes of his own. And Julien had already watched one parent die in front of him. King couldn't do that to him again. He balanced his weight onto his good leg, just in case he had to move fast. "Everything's going to be okay."

"The lies parents tell their children," Catalina said. "No wonder betrayal trauma has become so prevalent these days."

His son flinched at the comment. Or maybe from the woman's grip around his neck. King couldn't tell which, but one thing was clear. Nothing was going to stop him from getting Julien out of here alive. "Let me guess. You're here for the intel your husband handed over on your operation."

"You're smarter than you look, Agent Elsher." Catalina stepped fully into the ring of armed cartel members, putting Julien that much closer to the barrel of an assault rifle. "I'll make this easy for you. Give me what I want, and you and Julien are free to leave this place."

"While you burn Socorro to the ground." That wasn't an option. "Why? Why dump Adam's body at Socorro's doorstep? They didn't have anything to do with this until I approached them for help finding your husband."

"Is that what she told you?" A weak, sad smile creased crow's feet at the edges of Catalina's dark brown eyes. "Ivy Bardot knew about your partner's investigation long before you recruited Socorro into your little revenge plot, Agent Elsher. How else would he and that ATF agent access satellite images and intel about my operations over the years without raising federal suspicions? I imagine that's why she offered you her resources in the first place. Because once I took care of your partners, Socorro lost their hold in my dealings. And she couldn't have that."

Was that true? Had Ivy Bardot already known exactly who he was and what he wanted before he'd stepped into that conference room? Had she used him?

"Only now it seems I'm presented with the opportunity to take out two birds with one stone," Catalina said. "My uncle would still be alive if it weren't for Socorro. Metias raised me, you know. Taught me everything I know, made sure I went to the best schools, supported me. He shaped me into the woman I am today. One who's going to lead Sangre por Sangre into the future."

Blah blah blah. King didn't have time for this. Cartel reinforcements would only skew the chances he and Julien had of making it out alive. "Then I was right. You were the one behind taking out the other cartels in the area. Not your husband."

"Hernando served his purpose well. Kept the DEA and other federal agencies focused on him while I moved the deal with the triad forward," she said.

A ferocious growl resonated from the back of the armored truck, and Catalina let her hand slide from Julien's neck.

"It worked for a while." She backed toward the truck. "But after you and your friend—Scarlett is her name?—breached my warehouse, I discovered Hernando hadn't been as true to me as he promised in our wedding vows. And, well, I couldn't have that."

The widow motioned for one of the gunmen, and Gruber lunged from the darkness. A restraint prevented him from opening his mouth wider than a few centimeters while the choke chain kept him from attacking. The K9's dark eyes focused on Julien before the animal went wild all over again. As though he were trying to live up to his orders to protect King's son.

King locked his gaze on Julien. "Stay with Gruber."

His son's terrified face relaxed slightly.

"I've given you my terms, Agent Elsher." The widow was losing her patience, her voice icier than a moment ago. "But you seem to have come down here empty-handed. Am I to understand you won't be giving me what I came for and that I'll have to do to you what I did to the other two agents who crossed me? What were their names again? Eva Roday and Adam Dunkeld, right? Were they friends of yours?"

Rage bubbled up his throat. "You were there that night. The night Eva was killed. You ordered her murder."

"No, Agent Elsher," Catalina said. "That's one tradition I don't follow in the cartel. You see, I do my own dirty work."

Eva. Adam. Muñoz. This woman had killed them all.

The elevator pinged again, drawing the attention of every gunman in the garage.

"You might've gotten away with the murders of my partners, Catalina, but you're wrong about one thing." He heard the doors part. "I didn't come empty-handed."

Something hit the cement.

King didn't have to know what it was. He lunged for his son, securing Julien in his arms as the explosion rocked through the garage. Cement rained down on top of them as King rolled to put his son underneath his body.

Gruber's growl pierced through the cacophony of screams and gunshots, and King stuck a hand out. "Gruber!"

The K9 collided into King's back, every muscle the dog owned rippling in response to the attack. King loosened the choke collar from around the Doberman's neck and tore at the muzzle. *"Pass auf."* That was what Scarlett had said to get Gruber to protect Julien, and King needed the K9 on that job now more than ever.

A second bark registered from near the elevator, and a dark blur of lean muscle and sharp teeth burst through the circle of gunmen. Hans pounced on a soldier coming up on King and Julien, taking him down in a mess of claws and teeth.

King kissed the top of Julien's head. "Remember what I said, buddy. Stay with Gruber."

"Shoot them!" Catalina's voice was broken up by a series of coughs. Distant. In retreat.

King pushed upright as a glimpse of Catalina's white blazer disappeared into the back of the armored truck. The engine growled to life. "You're not getting away that easily."

Return gunfire cut through the haze of dust and debris still clouding the garage, and Scarlett shoved her way into the fight. She took aim at a soldier coming up on King's left and pulled the trigger. The gunman dropped. "Go! We've got this!"

It was then King realized she hadn't come alone. The operative who'd loaned King his vest rocketed his fist into a cartel member's face off to the left as another Socorro contractor unsheathed a knife from her cargo pants and sank it deep into an attacker's side. One by one they were picking off threats to give King the opportunity to finish this.

"Take care of my boy." He scratched behind Gruber's head, then ran for the armored vehicle. His leg protested every step, but he wasn't going to slow down. He wasn't going to let Catalina get away with what she'd done.

Her smile cut through the interior of the cargo area a split second before the door secured.

He ran into the two-inch steel and slapped his hand against the door. The vehicle lurched backward toward the entrance. "No!"

"King!" Scarlett's voice penetrated the haze of adrenaline and anger combining into a toxic cocktail under his skin.

He turned to face her just as she tossed him a brick of white clay. Only it wasn't clay.

King caught the mass and hurried to stick it under the armored vehicle's front wheel well. Catalina was in the passenger seat, that smile still in play. Until he unholstered his sidearm and took aim. Not at the windshield. At the brick of C-4 he'd planted on the armored truck.

He pulled the trigger.

The truck shot into the ceiling of the garage, the entire engine bursting into a thousand different pieces.

Strong hands grabbed the shoulders of King's Kevlar vest and dragged him to the ground. He slammed into the cement as a wall of gear and muscle and red hair shielded him from the blast. The explosion triggered a high-pitched ringing in his head, but through the aftermath, Scarlett's voice crystalized. "And you made fun of me for preparing for the zombie apocalypse."

Sirens screeched through the garage as two police patrol vehicles cut off the cartel's exit. The passenger side door of the armored vehicle fell open, depositing Catalina Muñoz onto the ground with a huff. Her white pantsuit would never be the same.

Nondescript SUVs skidded to a halt beyond the police wall and unloaded a dozen DEA agents, and Catalina had no other choice than to raise her hands in surrender.

The fight was over. King's son was safe. His leg would heal, and the world would keep turning. Without Eva and Adam in it. And all King could think to do was pass out cold.

Chapter Fifteen

Scarlett reset the ceiling tile in place.

Despite two explosions in the garage, her secondary defense system sat untouched. Everything was stable. Well, apart from the fact the entire building could suddenly collapse underneath her without warning. The engineers were working on it, and she'd have to remove the bricks of C-4 she installed through all four levels, but she wasn't able to stay away from this place. Socorro had become a home. A safe haven that'd given her life purpose after she'd thrown it away at the slightest misguided chance to do something good.

Only now she really had made a difference.

"Come on." She whistled low for Gruber to follow.

The K9 had followed her orders and protected Julien to the very end, taking a few samples of cartel member DNA in the process. There were more than a few gunmen sporting bite marks, and she'd made sure to give Gruber extra treats as a reward. Though it had been hard to separate him and Julien once the chaos of the attack had settled down. Even now, she was convinced the Doberman wanted to be with the kid instead of her.

Hans was still recovering from a broken rib sustained

during the fight in Muñoz's warehouse. Socorro's alarms had triggered her training to defend the team, but after reuniting with Gruber, the K9 finally seemed convinced that she could go to the vet clinic in Alpine Valley to serve out the rest of her recovery. And Scarlett made sure to check on her every chance she got between disarming the building so the construction crew could get to work.

As for Catalina Muñoz, her admission to killing Agents Eva Roday and Adam Dunkeld and her husband had been recorded on Socorro surveillance, which Scarlett had been all too happy to hand over to law enforcement. The medical examiner's office managed to collect a single sample of DNA from the blade stabbed into Adam Dunkeld's chest, and with a compulsory court order for a comparison, Catalina had written her own life sentence. Seemed stabbing a knife through an officer's badge took more strength than Catalina possessed. The blade had slipped, cutting her hand in the process.

Detectives had found a matching scar on her other hand, most likely from when she stabbed Agent Roday two months ago. Though they couldn't prove it, and Catalina wasn't talking to anyone without a lawyer.

Adding abduction charges on top of everything else had almost been too easy with eyewitness statements from the women in the front office of the school identifying Catalina as the woman who checked Julien out the day he went missing, as well as surveillance video from the principal. DNA comparison from the scene inside the freezer of Muñoz's restaurant matched that of Adam Dunkeld, and though they couldn't tie Catalina directly to the scene, her admission of the agent's murder was enough for the prosecutor. And charges filed by the DEA once they concluded their investigation into the fentanyl from the warehouse would ensure the widow never saw the outside of a prison ever again for what she'd done.

The triad was still a problem. Sangre por Sangre's newest partners had lost their supply line into the country, and from what little she knew of organizations like theirs, this wasn't over. They would try to reestablish contact, maybe take on a new liaison given they'd lost both Muñozes. If anything, Scarlett had the feeling the fight ahead would be much, much worse than what they'd survived this week.

But she wasn't fighting this war alone. Agents Roday and Dunkeld had given the feds a huge leg up now that Scarlett had been able to decode the ciphered notes. Identities of triad contacts from Muñoz, bank account numbers for deposits to Sangre por Sangre, operations that spelled out which competing cartels were targeted in the purge. It was all there.

Ivy Bardot had taken the intel straight to the Pentagon. Socorro would take the lead with the support of the DEA, ATF and the CIA to keep the triad off American soil. Though King's and Ivy's professional relationship had been put on hold since they'd learned of Ivy secretly funding his partner's off-the-books investigation. But maybe in this case, the ends had justified the means.

But best of all, King and Julien had been reunited once Scarlett's partner had been allowed to receive visitors in the hospital. The wound in his leg would heal if he actually stayed off his feet and followed his physician's orders, but Scarlett had the sense his recovery wouldn't go as smoothly as they hoped. King's suspension from the DEA hadn't been lifted despite solving

his personal investigation, and the man wasn't the kind
to sit still for long. Especially not with Adam's funeral
scheduled for tomorrow.

Scarlett hefted the container of C-4 and wiring she'd
ripped out of the ceiling tiles from the floor and headed
for the security office. It was a shame Ivy had made her
take it all down. Then again, with the team working out
of Alpine Valley's doublewide trailer-slash-police-sta-
tion, there wasn't much here left to protect.

Her steps faltered as the weight of that realization set
in. Everything looked the same, yet her entire world had
changed. There wasn't anything left for her to protect.

She shouldered into the security room. And froze at
the realization she wasn't alone.

Gruber huffed before circling the room and then lung-
ing at the ten-year-old boy standing off to the left of the
door. Traitor.

"You certainly know how to throw a party." King
twisted in her desk chair. As though he'd been waiting
for her all this time. Considering he couldn't get around
with a crutch, she bet sitting grated on his nerves. "What
do we got here? Bricks of C-4 and wiring. It's not much,
but we can sure as hell put on a show."

Her grip tightened on the edges of the box. "Aren't
you supposed to be recuperating under professional su-
pervision? I thought I told security not to let you out of
the hospital."

"Julien couldn't wait until I got out to see Gruber."
King's smile broke at one side of his mouth as he watched
his son and Gruber start wrestling. The Doberman was
gentle. More so than he'd ever been with Scarlett, and

she couldn't help but imagine they would be friends for a very long time. "See? How can I say no to that face?"

Scarlett set the box of explosives on the corner of her L-shaped desk. "Has he said anything about what happened?"

"Nah." King set his elbows on his knees, shaking his head. "I'm not sure he ever will, and I'm okay with that. When he's ready to talk to me—or to anyone else for that matter—I'll be there. I'm just happy to have him home."

"Right." That was what was important. That was what they'd fought so hard for. But the hollowness that had tried to break her so many times before wouldn't let go. They'd exposed a monumental shift within the Sangre por Sangre cartel, taken out one of their key players and managed to bring Julien home alive. She should've felt relief. Felt…something more than this deep ache that had set up behind her sternum the moment she partnered with King on this case.

"You weren't there. When I woke up." King raised his gaze to hers. "Hell, the last thing I remember before coming around in the hospital is you tackling me to the ground. The DEA came onto the scene, and then… I'm not even sure how I got out of there, but I knew who I wanted to see on the other side."

"Yeah." She clutched the handles of the box as though her life depended on it. She'd wanted to be there. At his bedside. She wanted to be the one holding his hand when his eyes opened and tell him everything was going to be okay.

But she'd frozen outside his hospital room, hand on the doorknob. The only thing she could hear were his final words cutting through her all over again.

The security monitors blurred in her peripheral vision. "There was a lot going on. I needed to coordinate with Alpine Valley PD and the DEA to make sure there were no other threats inside the building. And the engineers said they couldn't assess the damage until all explosives were removed off-site."

"Scarlett." King dragged himself out of the chair and shifted his weight onto his uninjured leg, somehow closing the distance between them. The room suddenly seemed so much smaller than before. "Granger told me what he uncovered while he was on assignment overseas. About the smuggling ring you were involved in."

Her throat constricted in defense, but she wasn't going to give him more to hold against her. Because he'd been right before. Admitting her involvement had given him everything he would need to have the army court-martial her and send her some place no one would ever find her. The DEA would come around. Sooner or later his suspension would be lifted, and King would be allowed to work in a federal capacity. With the power to destroy her and another member of her team.

"He told me you and your crew stole cash, weapons, drugs—anything you could get your hands on under the radar," he said. "He told me while the other soldiers you worked with were in it for themselves, you were the only one who took what you stole, turned it into cash and food and supplies and gave it to dozens of families stuck in their villages."

He put his hands on her. Soft at first, then tighter around her biceps, and she couldn't help but want that contact. To feel him holding her upright instead of her trying to hold up the entire world on her own.

"But even before Granger explained your involvement, I knew. In my heart, I know you're a woman who keeps her word. I know you were willing to risk your and Granger's freedom for my son, and I know there isn't anything you wouldn't do for the people—and the dogs—you care about. Even for the kid of a DEA agent who tackled you in a morgue."

Her burst of laughter took her by surprise.

"I was wrong, Scarlett. About everything. If it weren't for you, I wouldn't have my son back, and I owe you my life. I owe you more than that." King threaded one hand into the hair at the back of her neck, closing the last few inches of distance between them. "But most of all, I owe you an apology. Because I didn't mean what I said before. About you not meaning anything to me."

Her skin constricted around her bones. Too tight. "Oh?"

"The truth is, I was scared of caring about one more person after I've lost everyone in my life, and I ran at the slightest provocation," he said. "You carried me through this investigation. You saved me, and not just in that warehouse or downstairs in the garage. You kept me focused on what mattered, and you made me realize what I've lost is nothing compared to what's possible with you at my side. You mean everything to me."

Her mind automatically raced to fill in the blanks around that last statement, though she'd never been one to make a move while emotionally compromised. But she sure as hell wanted to start. "I'm going to need you to spell it out for me, King. And not on a camera without sound."

"All right. I love you." He traced his thumb along her

bottom lip, and a rush of sensation filtered through her system. "I used to think being a DEA agent was all I was worth, but now I know I'm meant to be your partner. In the field or out. I'm there for you. Whatever happens with my job and the suspension, wherever I end up, I don't care. Because I have everything I need right here in this…" he surveyed her dark corner of Socorro "…surveillance room."

"You love me?" Scarlett interlaced her hands behind his neck, drawing his mouth to hers. She was still trying to make sense of the past few minutes, but even off balance by the course of events and finding him in her security room, she hadn't felt this full in…ever. Whole. And yeah, she felt good, too. King had taken all those broken pieces she'd believed couldn't be put back together and shown her reality. "I love you, too."

"Ew!" Julien's protest broke through the bubble she and King had created around themselves, and Scarlett couldn't help but enjoy the sound of his voice for the first time.

She pulled back, swiping her hand across her mouth, and couldn't contain her laugh. Of all the times Julien could've broken his silence, she was glad to be part of it. "You're the one who wanted him to talk so badly."

"Sorry, buddy." King held on to her, and she caught sight of a line of tears reflected from the blue-white glow of the monitors. He'd been waiting for this moment for so long, and she couldn't help but feel that awe in his expression. "We'll try to behave ourselves."

Scarlett pressed her index finger into her partner's chest. "I guess now's a good time to tell you I've already drawn up plans to secure your house. Can't have the cartel or the triad coming for you or Julien again."

"Not with C-4, though." King studied the box not a foot from where they stood. "Right?"

Scarlett hefted the explosives off the desk to bundle with the three she'd already collected from the other floors.

"Scarlett." King followed after her. "Not with C-4."

"You said it yourself." She stacked the boxes together and dusted off her hands, getting a good look at Julien, King and Gruber. Her only wish was that Hans could be here with them, but the K9 would be up and running soon enough. And Scarlett couldn't wait for what came next. "I'll do whatever it takes to protect the people I care about."

* * * * *

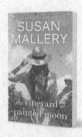